ON REFLECTION

D. M. ROSE

Author's Note:
The characters and institutions in this book cannot be found anywhere in real life. They and the situations they find themselves in are fictional. Nothing in this book is based on any existing individual, company or institution and any presumed likeness is purely coincidental.

ISBN 978-1-78003-848-3

Printed and published in the UK

Author Essentials Ltd
4 The Courtyard
South Street
Falmer
BN1 9PQ

A catalogue record of this book is available from the British Library

Cover design by Jacqueline Abromeit

Cover photo by D M Rose

CONTENTS

Other books by the author

The Storyteller
Death of Eternity
Another Country
Watching the World Go By
Fellow Travellers

STEPS TO HEAVEN

It was a glorious day as Eddie and Fred wound their way towards the bank surrounding the company's sports field. They could not have been more different in appearance. Eddie was a young slim woman in her early thirties, whereas Fred looked a good five years older, although he was, in fact, three years younger. Eddie was well turned-out, prim almost, and one of the company's high fliers. Fred was a grubby technical assistant, who the company would gladly have shed if they could have done so without paying him a redundancy settlement. High fliers, particularly female ones, were seldom popular, and Fred at least shared this characteristic with Eddie. He was almost universally loathed: he had a knack of saying the wrong thing at exactly the worst time. Worse yet from his colleagues' point of view, he'd got God. He was an evangelical Christian and he didn't mind who knew it. This had earned him a reputation as a hideous bore. Somehow, she couldn't quite think how, Eddie had managed to acquire Fred as a friend. He worked in a neighbouring department and often had to deliver messages and pieces of equipment to Eddie's department; in fact, do anything that would get him out from under the feet of his own colleagues.

They managed to find some shade under one of the trees which surrounded the sports field, and carefully disposed about them their shandies and plates of eggs, sausages and chips from the cafeteria. Eddie looked towards the cafeteria, where she could see Gerald and Paul, two of the senior executives, sitting in the blazing conservatory oven and downing their lunchtime stodge. She could imagine they were commenting on her and Fred. She didn't care; in a couple of months' time she would be in Europe, away from the posterior-pinching Gerald and the niffy Fred. She reflected that at least no one could call Gerald grubby. On the contrary, he was so aggressively scrubbed and over-deodorized that it was possible to smell his presence long before the man himself ever came into view. The fragrance was, like everything about Gerald, totally false.

Absently, Eddie started scratching her left arm. Her dermatitis was playing her up again. It seemed to be worse in the summer. "Your skin giving you trouble again?" asked Fred, with his usual degree of tact.

"Mm," replied Eddie. It always seemed so unfair that anyone as mucky as Fred should have perfect skin. By rights, he should have been covered in sores.

"You know I prayed for you last time, and you said it got better," continued Fred.

"That was very kind of you, Fred," muttered Eddie.

"You know, I'm sure if you came to our church, the pastor there could help you. We have healing services every week. Last week he cured an old lady with arthritis. I'm sure he could help you."

Eddie sighed: "Look Fred, I'm sure it's very kind of you to try and help me in your own way, but I've told you before, I'm not interested in religion. I don't believe in it," she added pointedly.

Fred took this rejection philosophically, and speared a piece of sausage and a chip. "Yeah, yeah. I can respect that. You're not ready to believe yet. That's OK." Eddie couldn't quite understand how it was that an otherwise inarticulate Fred always managed to turn everything on the subject of religion around and become verbally manipulative. "Anyway," he continued, "You won't mind if I pray for you again, will you?"

Eddie was just about to say she'd rather he didn't, when she thought: "I can't actually stop him praying for me if he wants to, and I suppose he means well." She said: "Oh well, if you want to Fred." Whereupon he did. In full view of the other diners in the sports field and the cafeteria, he got down on his knees, raised his arms to heaven, and started speaking gobbledegook. He called it speaking in tongues. Eddie was extremely embarrassed. She felt herself blush purple and her arm began to itch furiously. "Oh Fred, oh no." But he was too far gone to hear her.

"There now," he said after a few minutes. "You'll see, it'll get better. I'm sure Our Lord will help you." Eddie threw her sausages and chips down her throat and ungraciously muttered something about being late for her after-lunch meeting. Carrying her dirty plate, she almost ran back to the cafeteria. Behind her Fred was smiling beatifically.

Paul suavely welcomed everyone to the conference room. As well as Eddie, there was Alice, the senior designer, Will, the operations manager, Gerald, the sales supremo, and Mack, the financial manager. Eddie was interested to note that she was apparently not the only one to find Gerald overpowering. Despite his efforts to the contrary, he could find no one to sit next to him. Alice's sniff, as she stood up to fetch herself a cup of coffee, was almost derisory. Paul looked at her sharply, but he did not volunteer to sit next to Gerald himself, even if he was wearing the company's latest product.

Gerald was in his element. Today he was revealing his new plan to gee-up the sales force. Almost six months ago, Paul had decided that since the company's products were innovative and essential for every sophisticated human being in the western world, and since they were delightfully packaged and sold at very reasonable prices, the sales force was clearly failing to get retailers to stock and promote them. The problem had been as simple as that. Gerald was the solution. In his time, he'd sold insurance and bread, among other things. Now he was selling cosmetics and health and beauty products. Eddie only felt grateful he wasn't selling nuclear weapons, such was his zeal.

Gerald's ideas for improving sales performance were simple and direct. And, thought Eddie, likely to bring about the resignation of about fifty per cent of the sales force. Gerald quite simply proposed to do away with their basic salaries and put them all on a commission-only basis. In addition, he would institute a compulsory training programme for all, from the most junior to the twenty-year veterans. Mack wholeheartedly agreed with the commission-only idea. He was already calculating how much the company would save, but Paul could see a problem. "Yes Gerald, but you see they all have contracts of employment with us."

Gerald smiled, his all-over, "admire my private dentistry", smile. "Stipulating a certain volume of sales per month. Hardly any of them are doing that. I've checked. We can get rid of 'em easily enough. No sweat."

"And then what?" asked Alice acidly.

"We re-hire them on the new contract, or we get someone else, someone new."

Will chipped in his pennyworth: "For 'tis the American way. Except, of course, that we're not Americans. We do have some scruples about the way we treat our staff, I suppose. Or is that asking too much?"

Paul equivocated: "We certainly do have a good reputation for employee relations. It is, after all, the ground on which the company has always stood. Old Erasmus, when he first opened his factory…" Gerald yawned. "We've always had very good relations with our staff. We've never had union trouble or anything like that. And I do think it pays really. We get good staff because the conditions and perks are good, compared with our competitors. Besides, it gives us a good reputation with the public. Our products are regarded as good quality, wholesome, you know what I mean."

Gerald interrupted: "In fact, everything in the garden would be lovely, if only we could shift the stuff, but we can't. Our sales people know they're going to get paid whether they sell or not. So they don't. They've got no incentive."

"Perhaps if we were to offer an enhanced bonus system." Will was thinking aloud.

"Sorry, out of the question," said Mack. Gerald rolled his eyes.

"What do you think, Eddie?" asked Paul.

"Well, I don't think shafting a loyal sales force is the answer," she replied. "I agree with you, Paul. The company does have an image. It's been known as a progressive employer and manufacturer of good, dependable products ever since it was founded in 1883. That was part of Erasmus' philosophy, his practical religion, as he called it. If we once lose that reputation, we'll never get it back. The public will see us in just the same light as our French and American competitors. It won't do us any good. What we need, perhaps, are some more exciting products. Maybe when I get over to the lab. in Toulouse, I'll get some leads on that."

"I agree," chipped in Alice. "We've got the skills, we just need a bit of new input, some new ideas. That's why Eddie's here; let her do her job."

"And while you boffins are wasting your time, piddling about in the labs. we're all going bust." Gerald was getting quite ratty.

"We wouldn't want that, would we, Gerald?" asked Will quietly.

"And what is that supposed to mean?" It was a redundant question. They all knew the answer. Gerald had had what was discreetly known as a chequered history. Having eaten his way through the bread market, he'd taken to selling insurance, when, as he had assured Paul, he'd earned about £75,000 a year. The only trouble was that he'd spent it all. He'd forgotten to pay his taxes. As Mack was later to remark: "Not much of an advertisement for a financial adviser, so called." Consequently, Gerald had found himself in deep trouble and compelled to join the ranks of the employed, at a salary of considerably less than £75,000 to pay off the tax man.

Paul was beginning to look upset. Eddie thought it one of his more endearing characteristics: he hated rows. He really was a most unsuitable type for a company executive. If he hadn't been old Erasmus' great, great nephew, he wouldn't be. Irrelevantly, Eddie wondered what the old man would have done now. Paul did the only thing he knew how. He compromised, and invited Gerald to outline his training programme.

Nothing loath, Gerald started to unfold his flip charts. It appeared that sometime in his younger days, he'd been working for a multinational company which had sent all its sales people on a training course run by an ex-car salesman from Minneapolis. This guy claimed to have found the secret of happiness and fulfilment, and had developed a programme which, if rigorously followed, would enable his devotees to find the meaning of life and cope with all its problems and, incidentally, to give up smoking.

Gerald had been much impressed by this, and it was indeed true that he didn't smoke. One way and another, he had become quite a fan of Jack Shulz, and over the years had gone back for refresher courses and further training. He had even "qualified" in the "Jack Shulz School of Personal Enablement" and had been appointed to the rank of "chief moderator". At this point in his prepared speech, he nodded towards Eddie. After all, she was also another well educated and well qualified person, although her degrees, won after years of study, were not on a par with those from the Jack Shulz Academy. The pause, however, proved to be a mistake.

"What exactly does this course involve?" asked Will, with the emphasis on the word "exactly".

"How much?" asked Mack cynically.

"Oh God," was Alice's contribution. Eddie laughed and Paul looked hopeful. Gerald went on to explain that the course initially involved two weekends, usually spent in a hotel, somewhere with a suitable conference room, so the groups of around twenty participants would be able to concentrate on their personal developments, away from the worries of home and work. On the first day, the trainees were invited to think about, and discuss with their moderator, their past life traumas. There was later a session in which they were all invited to criticize one another. They would all be asked to fill out lists of their dreams, what they wanted from life. Gerald promised that during the second weekend the trainees would be shown how to obtain their goals. He didn't explain how.

Paul looked weary. "Yes, well, thank you, Gerald. A most interesting presentation. But really, while it's fine for… er… personal development, no doubt, I… er… don't really see how it gets the sales force to sell more of our products."

Gerald looked at him pityingly, but it was Will who replied: "The so-called moderator tells them that all their dreams will come true if they earn more money, and the way to do that is to sell more; right, Gerald?"

"Well, no not really. I mean I wouldn't put it in those terms. What we try to do is give them the inner security and confidence to deal with their day-to-day problems. Not just at work, but in their homes, with the wife and kids. It develops their personalities, gives them a new view on life. We teach them how to analyse themselves."

"And you're an example of this are you?" asked Alice, with no attempt to conceal her distaste.

"I must say, Gerald, it all sounds a bit vague to me," commented Paul.

"But it works. It really does work," enthused Gerald. "Jack Shulz runs courses for ABC and the new Euroexchange as well as for lots of American companies. This kind of executive training is all the thing now. You've got to move with the times. Give it a try. You'll see; it'll do wonders for the sales force."

"How much?" asked Mack again.

"Well usually the initial course costs around £800, but that includes hotel accommodation and meals and, of course, the fees for the moderator and the videos and copies of Jack Schulz's book."

"And the moderator in this case is you?" added Mack slyly.

Paul looked up, as though a light had just dawned on him. A light he didn't much like the look of.

"As a point of interest," asked Eddie, "is that it then? What happens when they've done the course?"

"When the trainees have made the initial discovery of the key to inner fulfilment, they go away and put it into practice. It improves their lives. I found, and I believe most people do, that once the initial discovery is made, it opens the way to even deeper understanding. "New Vistas" is what Jack Shulz called it in his book. There are more advanced courses, so that the followers can benefit throughout their lives. Even people who don't want to go any further often go back for refreshers, just the initial course again, you know."

At this point, most of the others were almost openly laughing, but Eddie could see something serious in it. "And you propose to make this a compulsory kind of training for all the reps?"

"Yes," replied Gerald flatly.

Paul woke up at last. "Well, if it will help, why don't we give it a try? There's nothing to lose, is there? We could do it over a couple of weekends, so that they're effectively doing it in their own time, and we could let them use the conference room here." Mack was about to protest about the cost, and Gerald was flashing his dental work and mentally calculating his profit, when Paul added: "And then, of course, we wouldn't have to pay a moderator. Gerald would be doing the training as part of his departmental responsibilities." Mack was relieved and Will snorted.

Gerald was about to start on about expenses, when Eddie interrupted him: "Sorry to be a fly in the ointment Paul, but there is a serious point here. As this is going to be compulsory, what we are, in fact, doing, is requiring the sales staff to undergo some sort of religious or philosophical training, which might be quite contrary to their personal principles, and which might be mentally harmful to them."

Alice quipped: "They're salesmen, they don't have principles."

Gerald retorted: "Rubbish!"

Paul looked non-plussed. "You mean it might be contrary to the ethical Christian basis of the firm?"

"Well, not just that," replied Eddie.

Mack interrupted: "I'm afraid I agree with Eddie, Paul. What Gerald is really talking about here is one of these modern-day therapy cults. They mostly come from America, and they all promise to enable you to solve life's problems and generally be a success, while at the same time finding the meaning of life. And they're all the same." Gerald started to shout angrily, but Mack continued: "And they are all cons, because the guys that start them up don't know what they're doing. They have some smart idea and then they market it and mentally break down their mug punters until they accept the idea and keep coming back for more. Because they're not trained…"

"Not trained? Not trained?" stormed Gerald. "I'm a graduate of the Jack Shulz Academy…"

Before he could get any further, Alice and Will started to laugh loudly. Even Paul smiled. "I hardly think, Gerald…" but he couldn't continue.

Will stopped laughing long enough to say: "Now that Mack has put it in that context, I think he's absolutely right. I remember reading about these types in the Sunday papers. Despite what Gerald may claim to the contrary, they do seem to have an unfortunate habit of causing alienation and mental breakdowns in their subjects. The whole thing seems very suspect to me. I think we should give it a wide berth."

"Oh God, yes," agreed Paul hastily. "We don't want to have anything to do with… er… well, anything like that. If it got round that we were brainwashing our staff, it would be the end of us."

"It's not brainwashing," reasoned Gerald, "and there are plenty of international companies who use this type of training for their executives as well as their sales forces. The Jack Shulz method is world renowned, and it's not a religion, just a way of helping people."

"But based upon Mr Shulz's own homespun philosophy," interrupted Mack.

"Yes, of course. After Jack had the "Realization" in Alabama in 1976, he thought he'd got a duty to tell the world about it."

Paul said: "No, I'm sorry Gerald. It was very kind of you to offer, but I don't really think it's the solution to our problems."

Gerald had one last try. "Eddie, you're a qualified scientist…"

"And you're not," she said firmly. "Neither are you a doctor or a psychologist. You're a salesman. Stick to that and don't mess with other people's minds. You're not qualified to do it."

In order to prevent the meeting breaking up in a slanging match, Paul compromised again: Gerald could advertise his course on the company noticeboard, and any members of the staff who wanted to attend could do so on a voluntary basis, in their own time, and at their own expense. To make it clear that the course was nothing to do with the company, they would have to hire hotel accommodation. Gerald could charge a nominal fee for his services. Afterwards, Paul would get feedback from the staff and they'd take it from there. In the meantime, they'd bring forward Eddie's departure for France. Gerald looked surprisingly happy with this arrangement, just like a salesman who'd got one foot in the door, until Mack said: "You can put me down, Gerald, I enjoy a good laugh."

From Eddie's point of view, one of the most unfortunate aspects of Gerald's contretemps with the Inland Revenue was that he had had to sell his palatial ranch bungalow and his wife and children, and now lived alone in a small detached house opposite her own. "Just slumming, you know, until I get the tax man off my back," he had explained to her on the day he had first offered her a lift home. Her secret fear was that it might take Gerald the rest of his life to get rid of the tax man. Since that first day, she had often thought it might be better to take the bus to work than endure twenty minutes of the awful Gerald twice a day. But then, she had an expensive mortgage and money was tight. Every little bit helped. On their way out of the factory that evening, they almost ran over Fred on his bike. "Oops, almost flattened your little friend," said Gerald maliciously. Eddie sighed. Roll on Toulouse.

Although she was looking forward to working in France, the rearrangement was not without its problems. For one thing, Eddie couldn't find a suitable tenant for her house while she was away. Her little property was considered inconveniently far from the town centre, and no one seemed to want a six months' lease. They all wanted something longer. In the tea queue the following morning, Fred sidled up to Eddie and asked brightly: "What you doing about your house when you go away, then?"

"Oh, I'm going to try and rent it out."

He thought about this for a few minutes, then offered: "Well, if you're looking for a nice quiet couple to look after the place for a few months, the new visiting pastor and his wife from our Church are looking for a short-term place to rent. Pastor Newland is coming up to retirement, and they're helping him out for a few months. By the way, I prayed for you last night; did you feel better?"

Eddie replied: "No, I'm afraid I can't say I did, Fred. You know you're probably wasting your time praying for me." She was just about to break off the conversation and head off to join Paul for tea, when an idea struck her. Why not rent her house out to this vicar and his wife? However awful their religion, it would at least mean they'd be well behaved. They couldn't afford any undesirable publicity. And Fred had said they only wanted a short-term let. It might be the answer to her prayers, if not to Fred's.

She said: "Well, you know, it might not be a bad idea for your pastor to rent my place for six months. It wouldn't be any longer than that, but I am looking for a respectable couple. It might suit us all."

"Great, thanks," said Fred. "They're only over here for nine months altogether and they want to do a bit of travelling before they go back to New Zealand, so six months should sit them just fine. They've been here a couple of weeks now, and they've been staying with Pastor Newland, but it's a bit crowded for them, so they're really keen to rent a little place. I've never been to your place," he added wistfully, "but I'm sure you keep it nice. And they would too, of course."

"Yes, I'm sure," said Eddie. "Look, here's my phone number; give it to them, and they can call and arrange to come round one evening." She wrote the number on a serviette and handed it to Fred. "And don't go and lose the number Fred and, whatever you do, don't give it to anyone, I'm ex-directory."

"Don't worry, I'll be careful with it."

Fred went off to sit with his fellow technicians, and Eddie found a place beside Mack. He looked at her very thoughtfully as she sat down. "You look pleased with yourself," he said cautiously.

"I am. I think I may have found someone to rent my house while I'm away."

"Not Fred!" he exclaimed.

"Oh no, not him," she laughed. "It's the new vicar and his wife from Fred's church. They're just visiting from New Zealand, so they only want a short let. It could be just the thing."

Mack toyed with the sugar for a minute or two, and then said slowly: "Don't think I'm interfering in your private life, I'm not, but you want to be careful of these evangelical holy-roller-type Christians. They're just as bad as the Jack Shulzes of this world. Worse, in fact, because they're harder to spot."

"What do you mean?" asked Eddie.

"Well," he continued hesitantly, "I've noticed, couldn't help doing really, that Fred always seems to be trying to get friendly with you. Now, apart from the fact that you're an attractive young lady, have you ever thought why that might be?"

"I suppose because I haven't the heart to openly insult him, like most people seem to. I know he isn't everybody's cup of tea, and he isn't mine, but I just can't be that ruthless."

"And very commendable too. Very kind. But you see it leaves you vulnerable to his approaches."

Eddie laughed. "No, there's nothing like that, Mack, I can assure you. The thought. Yuk."

"I don't mean that, Eddie. What I mean is that people often don't realize that these types have to evangelize their religion. They have to bring people in. There's a lot of pressure on them to do that. They're failing in their Christian duty if they don't save souls. It's a bit like Gerald and his daft, bend-your-mind philosophy, except that there's no money involved for courses. Later on, of course, if they get you hooked, you have to contribute towards the church."

"But you have to do that with any church," she objected.

"Yes, you do. Nothing wrong in that. Oh dear; I'm not making a very good job of this, but what I'm trying to say, is that they go out and bring in new recruits in a very aggressive way. And, well, you're a single, well-heeled lady in a good job. You'd be just the kind of person they want. So be careful."

Eddie thought about what Mack had said. It was true that Fred had rather latched on to her, but she had never thought there could be an ulterior motive in it. She'd thought he genuinely liked her because she was kind to him. It came as something of a shock to learn it might not be so but, of course, he was always on about religion and offering to pray for her. But then, he was always full of God. Everyone said so. She said: "Thanks for warning me, Mack, I'll bear it in mind. Anyway, I've certainly no intention of joining up. If I could rent the place to a respectable couple, it would be a godsend. Oops! And I haven't a lot of time now the trip has been brought forward. After all, I won't even be in the house, I'll be in France."

"True, true," replied Mack thoughtfully. "Just make sure you get rid of them when you come back. Don't have any contact with them other than purely business."

In the event, when Pastor Dennis and his wife called round later the same evening, Eddie was relieved to see how wholesome they looked. He was wearing slightly baggy corduroy trousers and a checked shirt, and Mrs Dennis was wearing a hideous straight, sleeveless floral dress. The puckering around the neck and one of the armholes indicated that she'd made it herself. Eddie showed them over the small house and offered them coffee. They expressed themselves delighted and said they would take care of the small rose garden. "It's just like we imagined the old country would be," explained Mrs Dennis. "We won't even need to use the second bedroom, so you can lock anything you want to in there," she added. Mrs Dennis, it transpired, was a schoolteacher currently doing temporary work at the local primary school. They had no children. Eddie was, at first, a little worried about the rent, but the Dennises accepted her highest figure without demur.

"We get an allowance from the Church," he explained.

After promising to get the rental agreement drawn up straight away, Eddie arranged for the Dennises to move in in two weeks' time. On the way out, they met Eddie's next door neighbour, Mrs Warburton, in her front garden, and Eddie performed the introductions. "Well, you know, young Miss Evans is such a quiet neighbour, we never know she's there; not like some people," said Mrs Warburton, nodding across the road.

They all looked in the direction of Gerald's house. There was a huge truck full of soil parked in the street, and a mechanical digger was parked in front of his neighbour's drive. "They've been at it all day, digging and banging about. Poor old Mr Johns can't even get his car out of his own drive."

"What's he doing?" asked Eddie.

"Digging his way to Wellington, by the look of it," quipped the pastor.

"He's having a swimming pool put in the back garden, if you please," answered Mrs Warburton.

"A swimming pool?" Eddie couldn't believe it. Gerald's garden was no bigger than her own. She couldn't imagine how anyone could get a decent sized pool in such a small plot. "He's digging out almost the whole garden; Mr Johns says there'll be only just about enough room to walk round the edges. All those lovely shrubs gone to waste." Mrs Warburton shook her head sadly.

"Well don't worry about us, Miss Evans, we won't be putting a pool in," smiled the pastor. Mrs Dennis smiled too.

On the way into work the following morning, Eddie couldn't help mentioning the new pool. "Yep; it'll be great in the summer. We used to have a pool up at Willowhaven. It's surprising how much you miss it," replied Gerald.

"But won't it be a bit small?"

"Sure, it'll be smaller than I'm used to, but I'll be able to swim good lengths, even if it is a bit narrow. Good for the heart, swimming. You must come over and try it when you get back." Gerald gave the dental work another airing, and looked wolfishly at Eddie.

"It's certainly causing a bit of a stir among the neighbours," she replied. "I thought you weren't planning to stay that long. I mean, is it really worth going to all that trouble and expense?"

"It's no trouble."

"Not to you, maybe."

"No, it's no trouble at all, and I'm getting it at cost. The guy is a friend of mine. Mates' rates. So if you ever want a pool, tip me the wink and I'll get you a good deal. He breathed all over Eddie. Not only was it deodorant, now it was killer mouthwash. She shuddered.

"It's a pity you're going away so soon," he said. "You'll miss the enabling course. It starts the day after you leave. I'm sure you'd find it interesting. I've already booked the hotel." He paused meaningfully "When you get back, eh?"

The awful thing about Gerald, apart from the deodorant,

was that he never gave up. He never took "no" for an answer. Eddie supposed this was what made a good salesman. "You know what I think about that sort of crap, Gerald. I wouldn't touch it with a bargepole. It's just a con for making a load of money for Jack Shulz, and you're daft to go along with it. I'm surprised you can't see that."

Gerald shook his head. "Not at all, you've got it all wrong. You've just got a closed mind. Nobody makes any money out of it."

Eddie laughed aloud. "Except you, when you run those courses, and I suppose a percentage of that goes to Shulz."

"I'm only being paid for my time," he said defensively, "and the materials we give to the trainees, Jack Shulz's book and the videos, you'd expect to pay for them, naturally."

"Don't you understand, Gerald, it's dangerous? You're messing about with people's minds, their personalities. That can be psychologically damaging."

"Never did me any harm. Thanks to Jack Shulz I feel I can do anything I want. Life is just a stream of exciting challenges. No worries, no problems, just challenges. Positive thinking. You could do with a bit of that, you know."

"At least the fees you'll get from the mugs will help you pay off the Inland Revenue," said Eddie nastily.

Two weeks later Eddie departed for fun and sun in the south of France, leaving the boring Pastor and Mrs Dennis duly installed in her home, Gerald busily organizing his con trick, and the evangelical Fred still praying for her dermatitis.

A few weeks later, Eddie received her first letter from Mack. He'd been to Gerald's weekend and gleefully recounted to her what a disaster it had been. Apparently, someone, no names, but someone she knew, had been round telling some of the sales staff and the younger managers that Gerald was organizing a con trick at their expense. Consequently, half of the would-be trainees failed to attend and, more importantly, had failed to pay their fees, so Gerald had got saddled with a large bill for accommodation and catering from the hotel. It was rumoured he would probably not break even, even when he'd taken out the cost of the Jack Shulz books and videos he'd bought for the trainees. "Over confidence," wrote Mack. "Gerald made and paid for all the arrangements, never thinking that he'd have anything less than a full course." Worse yet, from Gerald's point of view, was the fact that Pat from the typing pool, having paid her fees, had gone down with flu. Gerald had refused to refund her money, and so, to spite him, she allowed Fred to go in her place. Eddie read that Fred had provided the sensation of the course. Right in the middle of the second morning, while Gerald was telling the trainees how Jack Shulz and his ideas could help them solve all their problems, Fred had stood up and announced that Shulz and his like were inspired by Satan and that all the ideas Gerald was so assiduously promoting were demonic. Then, to make matters worse, Fred had actually read for about five minutes from the Book of Revelation.

Eddie could just picture the scene: she didn't need Mack's description to envisage Fred reading from the Bible, Gerald shouting at him, and everyone else falling about laughing. All in all, Mack admitted to having had a very good time. "Worth every penny I paid for it," was his conclusion. Not that he had actually paid. On the grounds that the course wasn't finished as promised, he'd stopped his cheque at the bank. Gerald had become a laughing stock, particularly amongst his own sales teams. Paul was considering Gerald's position within the company. Certainly there was no prospect of him ever being allowed to run Jack Shulz Enabling Courses again, and Paul had finally rejected his proposal to put the sales force on commission-only. It was rumoured that Gerald wasn't going to get his productivity bonus, and he'd been seen mooching around the office, moaning about not being able to pay for his new pool.

The letter Eddie received from Mrs Warburton a month later was much less welcome than Mack's had been. The poor old lady seemed to be at the end of her tether. She knew it wasn't Eddie's fault, but she rued the day the house had ever been rented to those awful New Zealanders. She asked pointedly when Eddie was likely to be coming home. The problem, it seemed, was that Pastor and Mrs Dennis had taken to holding church meetings in Eddie's home. According to Mrs Warburton, there were cars coming and going all day on Sundays and in the evenings when they had Bible study classes. This she could stand, at least for a few months. She could even endure being asked to join the Dennises in reading the Bible two or three times a day. It was the baptisms which were the last straw. The pastor and his wife had bought a bath and installed it in Eddie's back garden. New recruits to the church were baptised by total immersion in the bath. As Mrs Warburton wrote: "It goes on all day long, not like a normal baptism in church. They're all out there singing hymns and playing the guitar. Then they have a sermon, and they all shout 'Praise the Lord' and 'Hallelujah'." It was making her Stanley quite ill. She'd phoned the council about the noise, but they hadn't done anything.

Eddie was cross. She liked Mr and Mrs Warburton. They were old people. They didn't deserve to be upset like that. The Dennises were flagrantly breaking their understanding with her. They were abusing her goodwill in renting the house to them in the first place. She wrote a nice letter back to Mrs Warburton, promising to remind the Dennises of the terms of their lease, and to the Dennises she wrote a much sharper letter, asking them to refrain from using her home for church business. The Dennises didn't even bother to reply; they got Fred to do that for them. He reminded Eddie that he was still praying for her, that the Dennises were carrying out God's work and that the Warburtons were welcome to join them any time they liked.

At the same time, Eddie received another letter from Mack. Everyone was fine back at the company and they were all missing her. Everyone except Gerald, that was. Gerald had apparently gone mad. He was in yet more trouble with the Inland Revenue and had taken to drink. More than once Mack had seen him nipping out to the pub down the road at lunch time, and the smell of deodorant had been replaced by that of stale alcohol. In an effort to redeem himself and prove his worth, he had decided on his own programme to gee-up the sales force. It consisted primarily of violently losing his temper with them every time they came back into the office without making a sale. Mack related that several of the male staff had complained to Paul, and one of the female reps. had been reduced to tears. However, there was one good piece of news: Fred was leaving. He was going to train as a pastor for his church. "So at least when you get back, you won't have him in your hair." So far, Eddie hadn't confided in Mack about her problems with the Dennises, and she decided not to do so now. There was nothing he could do. Instead, she contacted her solicitor concerning the terms of their lease.

Mrs Warburton wrote again: the neighbours had got up a petition to the council, complaining about the noise and the use of her house for non-residential purposes. She was sorry, but they simply couldn't stand any more. She hoped it wouldn't cause any trouble for Eddie. In fact, Eddie was quite glad. The petition should enable her to get rid of the Dennises more easily. She'd quite happily lose the rent in order to have her house back. She was beginning to think about Mack's warning: supposing they just refused to budge when she returned home? She'd have to drag them through the courts, and how long would that take? She had visions of herself living in an expensive hotel while they used her home as a church. She barely noticed the line in Mrs Warburton's letter that said: "Oddly enough, that yuppie man with the swimming pool, the one who works with you, refused to sign the petition." Indeed, Mrs Warburton reported she'd seen him laughing and joking with the pastor in the street one evening, and he'd also been over to their house in the evenings.

At about the same time as Eddie received a reply from her solicitor, outlining her legal options and enclosing a copy of a letter he'd received from the Dennises, she also received a phone call from Paul, asking her to return to the office for a week. They had a minor crisis on their hands: the sales staff were threatening to walk out *en masse*. Gerald had stopped trying to re-programme their brains and had stopped losing his temper with them. Instead, he was now doing something far worse. He was insisting they all be in the office at nine sharp every morning for a short prayer meeting and to listen to a reading from the Bible. While Paul appreciated Gerald's efforts to involve the deity on the company's behalf, he himself felt it wasn't right to bother God about business worries, and one or two of the sales force who were not Christians positively resented Gerald's efforts. Even those staff who were, remained unimpressed by Gerald's Hell-fire ecstasies. Eddie promised to get everything wound up by Friday afternoon and be on the evening shuttle back to London.

She glanced again at her solicitor's letter. It was more or less what she expected. It was the reply from the Dennises which caught her eye. Phrases like "Inspired by Satan" and "Servitor of Mammon" leapt up at her, coupled with promises for a miserable, if warm, eternity for those who tried to halt the spread of God's word. Apparently these strictures were also to be applied to their solicitors. At least she wouldn't be alone in Hades. She wondered if Mrs Warburton would be there too. On impulse she phoned Mack for the low-down on Gerald. "Yep, it's all true. Jack Shulz is out. God is in. In a big way."

"How on earth did he get involved? I mean I know he lives across the road from that pastor I rented my house to, but surely there's more to it than that?"

Mack unfolded the tale. After the disastrous weekend course, which Fred had done so much to destroy, Gerald had been feeling humiliated and depressed. He'd made a fool of himself and his money troubles were mounting. Fred, spotting a vulnerable victim, with the unerring eye of an eagle searching for prey, had befriended him. It had been but a short step to explain to Gerald that his life was in a mess because he was following Satan's path. If he were to follow Jesus, everything in the garden would be lovely. The sales team would sell like mad if God was behind them, and the staff of the Inland Revenue would be struck by lightning, "or something like that," added Mack. So Fred had invited Gerald to visit the Dennises. After a few visits, he'd decided to join up and had been baptised, and that was it. "He just dropped one crutch and picked up another."

"Oh dear," said Eddie. "I feel guilty for having rented them my house in the first place. They've been nothing but trouble, you know."

"You're not responsible for what they're doing," said Mack "I take it they are breaking the terms of their lease. I don't suppose you specifically allowed them to turn your house into a church? And it doesn't much matter where they live, they'd be doing the same thing anywhere. In any case, it was that awful Fred who got him hooked in the first place, and he did that through their acquaintanceship here. Just be grateful he didn't get his hooks into you."

Eddie explained she was taking steps to have the Dennises evicted, so, hopefully, that might get them away from Gerald.

Eddie arrived in England late on Friday. Before going to the hotel booked for her by the company, she took a taxi back to her home. As the cab rounded the corner of her street, she was greeted by a sight that looked like something out of a television film shoot. Mr and Mrs Warburton were in the middle of the road, talking to a lugubrious man in a mackintosh, who was obviously a police officer. There was a police car partially blocking the road. Mr Johns was sitting on his own front garden wall, talking to a young PC. Eddie paid off the taxi, put her luggage on the pavement next to the police car, and went up to the Warburtons.

"Here she is," she heard Mrs Warburton say. Before the police officer could introduce himself, Mrs Warburton exclaimed: "Oh Miss Evans, thank goodness you're here. It was awful. Horrible. Poor Mr Johns nearly had a heart attack. They've had the doctor to him, but he won't go to hospital."

"Whatever is the matter, Mrs Warburton?" asked Eddie.

It was Pastor Dennis, appearing from behind her own hedge, who answered: "He lost faith. He failed to believe, and God took him."

"What!" exclaimed Eddie.

"The gentleman in number twenty-four, Mr Gerald Price; I believe he was a friend of yours, Miss Evans?" asked the policeman.

"Well… er… we worked together." Eddie was not keen to claim Gerald for a friend, even in death.

"And you have rented your house to Pastor and Mrs Dennis here?"

"More's the pity," she replied.

"Quite so, Miss Evans. Quite so. Well it all seems fairly plain." Eddie was completely mystified.

"It was murder," screeched Mrs Warburton. "That's what it was. Nothing short of murder. Telling him he could walk on water, if you please."

"He must have been daft," put in her husband.

"He was following in the footsteps of Our Lord," said the pastor. "And he lost faith. His faith wasn't strong enough, and he was contaminated by the demon alcohol." Mrs Dennis came up to join the group.

"He was doing what?" Eddie couldn't believe it.

The police officer explained that Mr Price had recently become a member of the "Church" run by Mr Dennis in Eddie's home.

"Pastor," corrected Mr Dennis loudly.

The police officer continued: convinced of the power of God, which was protecting and guiding him. Mr Price, after consuming three quarters of a bottle of wine (1.5 litre size) had decided to test his faith by walking on water. To be precise, by walking across his own, unpaid for, swimming pool. He'd drowned. Mr Johns had heard a noise and gone out into his own back garden, seen Gerald floating face down, and called the emergency services. In the event, they had been of more use to Mr Johns than to Gerald.

Pastor Dennis started to preach again: "He was falling into the sin of pride…"

"To be exact, sir, he fell into his own swimming pool," interrupted the police officer.

"He was falling back into Satan's clutches, as will all who try to thwart us in our mission." Having delivered his message, the pastor stared pointedly at Eddie.

"Go to Hell," she said, "and before you do, get out of my house."

By now the local press had arrived to photograph and interview all and sundry. The consequent adverse publicity did in days what would have taken the courts months to achieve: Pastor and Mrs Dennis removed themselves from Eddie's house three days later. The only problem was that she was left with the bath in the back garden. And her dermatitis was itching like the plague.

"You don't realise how mean he really is," said Susie. "He even accompanies me round the freezer centre to make sure I get the cheapest available brands."

"Oh, I'm sure he's just doing it to help you with the weight," replied Ken in his lovely transatlantic accent.

Susie had always liked Ken, who was a widower; he was unfailingly courteous and obliging and never showed how miserable he really was. She wished she could do more to help him but, as Malcolm said: "Business is business." "So that's it then. Three messages from yesterday afternoon, and none of them from Jacobs Brothers," she said.

"Oh well, thanks anyway," replied Ken, as he plodded into the main open plan office to begin his morning phone session.

"Any business this morning?" shouted Malcolm, who was Susie's husband and the senior team manager in the office.

"Afraid not," shouted Ken.

"Well, keep at it," exhorted Malcolm, as he returned to his own glass panelled room.

Ken sat down to return the calls from the previous afternoon and pulled his meticulously written phone list from his briefcase. He'd got a local trade directory and was ploughing through all the local small businesses to see if they needed insurance or pension schemes for their employees. Occasionally he got lucky. Mostly he didn't. He hated doing this. It was such a come down. Only two years ago he'd been in Chicago as the export manager of a British company there selling customized luxury fitments for cars. But then the recession had come, and it had hit the American market particularly badly. The company had simply closed down its American operation and fired all the staff. Sure, he'd got a good redundancy package; he'd been with the company for twenty years after all; but with the cost of relocation to the UK and setting up house and the burden of being self-employed with no regular income, it had almost all gone. He was going to have to bring in more business, and soon, or he'd go bust. He wished he could be like Bernard.

Bernard, wearing a natty blazer, had just strolled into Susie's office in his leisurely way. Ken watched through the glass partition as Bernard picked up a sheaf of telephone messages. "How does he do it?" wondered Ken, not for the first time. Bernard, after all, did none of the activities that the other reps. did to generate business: he didn't spend hours on the phone like Ken; he didn't attend exhibitions or take stands in shopping centres; he certainly didn't do any personal canvassing; but he still got the leads to the new clients, the all-important introductions or enquiries from potential customers. By now Bernard had strolled into Malcolm's office and produced a pile of completed application forms. More business, more commission. And, naturally, Malcolm was pleased; he also received a percentage of the commission from the company. Malcolm checked the paperwork to see that it was all complete and that the necessary cheques were in order, and said he would pass them all on to admin. to be recorded in the ledgers and passed on to head office.

Yes, there was no doubt about it, Bernard was doing phenomenally well. He usually earned about £4,000 commission a month. He was the only rep. in the office who did, and he'd only been with Johnson-Williams about a year. But, of course, there were special reasons for his success. Bernard, who was a slightly portly individual of late middle age, with the sallow complexion that indicated years spent in sunnier climates, had once been a senior officer with the Hong Kong Police before returning to the UK. He and Malcolm had found an almost instant kinship, based on greed. Malcolm had formerly been a naval officer, and was roughly ten years older than Bernard, but his history after the Navy had been less successful than Bernard's. He'd run a small boat building business which had gone bust and, although he'd managed to pay all his creditors in full, he had found himself halfway through life without a penny to his name. It was then that he'd started as a rep. with Johnson-Williams, and had gone from strength to strength. Johnson-Williams was a very upmarket company, dealing with the financial requirements, both personal and business, of the better class of client. It even had its own banking and stockbroking concerns. Malcolm's military bearing had stood him in good stead when advising clients on investment and pension plans. He looked trustworthy; it was an honour to buy from him.

Even so, before Bernard had come on to the scene, Malcolm had been facing a not very-well-provided-for retirement himself. He still had a huge mortgage and a bank loan for the purchase of his yacht, and he was not, by nature, thrifty. Unlike his clients, he hadn't bothered to get a pension plan. But he did have his ability to sum up men. And, as he remarked to Susie, "One thing years in the colonies teaches a man is how to spot real wealth and the true value of corruption." Perhaps they were two things, but together they formed the basis of Bernard's success story. As Bernard had said, "With Susie working in reception, what could be simpler?" What indeed? Any potential customers who walked into the office or who phoned in response to the company's newspaper advertisements were gently questioned by Susie and most of the rich ones set aside for Malcolm's consideration. The time-wasters and the poorer clients were fairly distributed to the other two team managers. They knew what was going on and had complained to head office about having Susie in reception. But they had no proof, and Malcolm had so many friends in the higher echelons of the company that his position was unassailable. If the other managers didn't like it, they were welcome to try their luck elsewhere. They often did; there was quite a turnover. What even the other managers had not guessed was how Malcolm distributed the leads within his own team. When Bernard had proposed an extra 20% commission for Malcolm out of his own commission and on top of what the company allowed, Malcolm had had no hesitation in passing on to Bernard all the best leads.

Bernard had explained it all to his charming Eurasian wife, Marguerite. "It's no more expensive than paying for exhibitions or adverts, it takes less time, the clients are richer, and it's better to have 80% of something than 100% of nothing." Even Malcolm's mercenary soul had wondered about a man who could marry a woman as beautiful as Marguerite for her money. Undoubtedly she had money: she had bought their house outright and, in true oriental fashion, had allowed Bernard to have his name alone on the deeds. Still, she was not without her drawbacks, and Bernard was hard put to to keep her in the clothes and antiques she seemed to gobble up; and now she'd discovered the golf and yacht clubs, there was no holding her. It was part of their bargain: she'd put up the capital, Bernard had to see to the maintenance of her lifestyle.

Fortunately, it was going to be another good month for Bernard. Not so for Colin, at 28, one of the youngest reps. in the office. Malcolm had had grave reservations about taking him on. He really didn't fit the upmarket image of Johnson-Williams, but he had come at a time when they were desperate for new recruits. At first everything had gone well enough. Colin was a local man with a seemingly inexhaustible supply of drinking companions and golf partners. Malcolm couldn't really picture Colin playing golf. He only ever saw him in his immaculate striped suit and red braces, doing an imitation of one of those American films Susie was so keen on. The trouble was that Colin was personally financially irresponsible, and so were the friends he did business with. After a month or two, they stopped their premiums, and the commissions were taken back by the company. All that was achieved was a lot of wasted time spent on Colin's beer-stained paperwork. Worse yet, Colin didn't like Bernard and, as he was a very street-wise type, Malcolm wondered if he'd guessed what was going on. For that reason, he occasionally found himself slipping good leads to Colin instead of Bernard. It was a waste, because Colin simply couldn't deal with upper class people. He never got the business. The clients regarded him as a spiv: what Malcolm would call a wide-boy. Judging by the way Colin was avoiding looking in the direction of Malcolm's office, last night had been another failure.

And talking of failure, there was Bill again, shuffling into reception. Bill looked like every man's idea of a down-at-heel insurance salesman: cheap off the peg suit, scuffed suede shoes, spotted tie, and none too fresh cream shirt. He wore the lugubrious expression of the permanently worried. He was. His wife nagged him, the mortgage was in arrears, and the kids were facing the imminent prospect of state schooling, instead of the private establishment they now went to. The silly thing was that he'd been a salesman of electrical equipment before joining Johnson-Williams. He'd managed then, done quite well by all accounts, but financial services just wasn't his thing; he was a fish out of water. After collecting his messages, he trundled into Malcolm's sanctum with the business from last night: a £20 per month pension plan for a forty year old. "One thing," thought Malcolm, "at least his paperwork isn't bad." He said: "Good, keep it up, you're beginning to get the business in now, but you need more of it; be consistent, work to a plan." Bill smiled sadly. He'd heard it all before. He did work to a plan: telephoning and doing personal canvassing. He worked damned hard. But all he ever got from Malcolm was verbal encouragement; he never got any of the leads.

"How much have I got this month?" he asked.

"About £800," replied Malcolm, checking his ledger, "If we can get this issued in time."

Bill plodded off into a corner of the open plan office. Knowing admin. as he did, he knew it wouldn't get issued, so he wouldn't get the commission until next month. Anyway, that part time job Mary had found for him as a barman down at the marina on weekends and evenings would come in useful. The wages weren't much, but the tips were supposed to be good.

Susie brought in Malcolm's morning tea and biscuits. "It's that Earl Grey tea Angela from admin. got," she said.

"If Angela wants the office to have Earl Grey, let her buy it," replied Malcolm ungraciously. "Cheapo-save's floor sweepings is good enough for that lot." Susie's phone rang, and she ran out before she had time to remonstrate with Malcolm over his meanness. At the other end of the line was someone who could barely speak English, but fortunately the caller did manage to make it clear that he wanted to speak to Bernard. The call was duly transferred and the office was treated to the unusual sound of Bernard speaking Chinese.

As lunchtime approached, the reps. started drifting out to local pubs or cafés before going on to afternoon appointments, and Susie went shopping. Malcolm sat in his office, masticating home-made cheese sandwiches and flicking through his yachting magazine. His eyes rested on an article about the prevalence of theft and the disguising of stolen yachts. Owners were instructed to beware and take security precautions. It was not at all rare for yachts to be sailed to Spain, re-named, and sold within a couple of weeks. The *Current Seas* was a great extravagance and accounted in part for Malcolm's petty meanness. Moored at the marina, she was undoubtedly one of the most expensive yachts there, and Malcolm had had to borrow heavily from the bank to buy her. But, as he had said to Susie, she was an investment. It was good for business to have a high social profile, and they could entertain upmarket clients on board and, with any luck, pick up a few more from the yachting community. If things got really tight, they could always rent it out for cruises. Malcolm still loved the sea, and in many ways he regretted leaving the Navy so early. The sea was another thing Malcolm shared in common with Bernard: he'd spent a lot of time on the water in his days in Hong Kong.

Two days later, Bernard sauntered into Malcolm's office and closed the door behind him. He drew a chair up close and said: "I suppose Susie told you I got a phone call a couple of days ago from a Chinese?"

"I noticed it myself," replied Malcolm. "Well, here's something that could be good for both of us, in a big way." Bernard smiled. "That was Mr Chin from Hong Kong. I knew him when I was out there, and he's loaded, even by their standards. And so are the rest of his family. But post 1997 he's decided to clear out. Most of his younger relatives have gone already and, as he's a widower, there's nothing left to keep him there, so he's winding up his business dealings and coming to retire in the mother country. Him and his money."

"How much?" asked Malcolm, who never believed one could be too crude in business.

"Well, by the time he's fixed himself up with a small palace full of antiques and a Roller, I reckon there'll be about two million left to fritter in investments."

"Are you sure you're going to get the business?" queried Malcolm.

"Oh yes, definitely," replied Bernard. "I took him out to lunch yesterday and he told me it's mine. He trusts me from the old days," he said, smiling a little so that Malcolm would understand. "You know how these people are; they're unfathomable, and you never really get to know them, but they put great store by personal friendship and they stick to their word, especially in business." Malcolm's eyes began to water as he absently tried to figure out the likely commission on a portfolio of investments for two million. And then there would be extra business from the family…

But then a nasty thought crossed Malcolm's mind: suppose Bernard double-crossed him about their arrangement. After all, this wasn't small fry, and it didn't come from a lead he had given him. If Bernard did decide to rip him off, there was very little he could do about it. He could hardly complain to head office, and if he suspended the arrangement, he would be the loser: no one else could bring in the upmarket business like Bernard. As if reading his thoughts, Bernard said: "Well, of course, our normal arrangement will apply, but since this is a personal contact of mine and not an office lead, I'd like you to help me in a practical way, if you would?"

"Sure," enthused Malcolm, "Anything I can do to make it go smoothly."

Bernard explained that Mr Chin was a very private individual and was staying in the UK for a few weeks while he looked out a suitable house. Having made a deposit from his bank account on Jersey, he would return home to Hong Kong for the final winding-up of his affairs, and then come to this country permanently. He had kept in touch with Bernard since he left the police and was, indeed, partly responsible for Bernard's decision to join Johnson-Williams. He had been very satisfied by the discreet way their banking arm had handled his account on Jersey. Not that he kept much in it, just about 100,000, prudently put by for the rainy day when the communists came. Just enough for the deposit on a house. In the meantime, Mr Chin was staying in a local hotel, having decided he would like to live in the south-east of England, within easy reach of London, and was setting out each day to explore the possibilities. He did not, however, like the hotel life; it was too public for his refined taste, and Bernard wondered if it would be possible for Mr Chin to stay on Malcolm's yacht at the Marina.

If Malcolm was a little taken aback by this odd request, he tried not to show it. He enquired how Mr Chin would manage alone on the yacht. Bernard assured him there would be no difficulties whatsoever; Mr Chin had made some of his fortune in shipping, and was accompanied by a poor-relation chauffeur-valet-cook already resident in this country. Malcolm agreed to Bernard's proposal and arranged to meet Mr Chin on board the yacht that evening. When Bernard had left his office to resume his normal duties of raking in the money from less illustrious clients, Malcolm put through a call to the Jersey banking office. Like the rest of the company, he had friends there. Without, naturally, going into details, they were able to reassure him that Mr Chin had had a substantial deposit with them for 18 months.

That evening was a balmy summer's evening, such as only the south coast of England can produce, with a warm on-shore breeze and the promise of a beautiful sunset. Malcolm was dressed in a suitably casual-elegant boating outfit as he fussed around the yacht, making sure everything was in order. A naturally fastidious man, who kept the yacht immaculate inside and out, Malcolm found very little that was not pleasing to the eye. He had prudently left Susie at home. She was a good girl and very attractive and kind, but he had to admit she really didn't have class. He had always been slightly ashamed of her, especially when he was in the Navy. It was a good thing she'd never fussed him about business, even when they'd gone bust, and she'd expressed no curiosity when he told her he had a business meeting with Bernard on the yacht.

At length, Bernard drove up in his Jaguar with a small, sparkling Chinese beside him. Marguerite was away visiting her mother, who had recently had a hip-replacement and needed help getting around the house. During the introductions, Malcolm took in the luxury of Mr Chin's slacks and blazer and the single diamond signet ring he wore. Over drinks and canapés, Malcolm showed Mr Chin around. The Chinese whose English was surprisingly poor for an international businessman, graciously smiled and attempted to praise everything he saw. Finally, he asked Malcolm about the financial arrangements. Malcolm cursed his own generosity and waved the subject away with a polite wrist movement. "Look upon it as an investment," he told himself.

"But of course," said Mr Chin softly, "I could not accept your hospitality without suitable… er… er… recompense." He seemed overjoyed to have found the right word. Malcolm looked at Bernard, who merely smiled blandly. Mr Chin named a very generous sum. Malcolm protested, but not too much. "After all, is it not said greed is good?" asked Mr Chin with a laugh. Malcolm had found a kindred soul; he smiled broadly. Mr Chin was obviously a cultured man; Malcolm had heard that phrase before. "Greed is good". The Bible wasn't it? How did it go? "Blessed are the rich, for they shall inherit."

The days broadened into a fortnight, as Mr Chin pursued his dream house. He kindly invited Malcolm and Susie on to the yacht for real Chinese meals, cooked by his relative. Bernard kept a low profile, but was known to accompany Mr Chin during his prospecting trips. A suitable property was finally found, left over from the days when it had housed "The Mind-Force Therapy Cult". Immediate vacant possession was assured by the fact that the cult leader was now in jail, along with several members of his entourage. The cult had, of course, been little more than a money-breeding programme. The end had come when the residents of the mansion had kidnapped an Inland Revenue inspector and subjected him to some of their programmes. The hapless inspector had, however, a very strong mind of his own, and had escaped after a few days. Not only were the powerful minds now in prison, but the Revenue had bankrupted them by adding back taxes. Mr Chin, in view of the unfortunate history of the house, and its "bad fortune", politely beat the price down to rock bottom. On the drive back to the coast Mr Chin asked Bernard: "Is there really a need for these new religions here? I have heard of them in America, but in Europe?" Bernard thoughtfully assured him there was. They remained in silence for the rest of the journey.

Bernard kept Malcolm abreast of Mr Chin's progress and continued to prosper himself. Malcolm instructed Susie to start buying cheaper cuts of meat and waited anxiously. Bill struggled on with both his jobs, Colin continued to drink away most of his earnings, and Ken became more watchful.

At a last lavish, catered meal aboard the yacht, a boys' night out, Mr Chin announced that on the morrow he would instruct the Jersey bank to transfer funds for his deposit to the solicitors acting for the vendors of the mansion. He intended to return to Hong Kong the following day and to return in about three weeks to attend to the completion of the sale and to start buying antiques. Never one to miss a chance, Malcolm asked Mr Chin if any of his relatives were now in this country, perhaps even some of his old friends and business acquaintances? Mr Chin replied that most of his younger relatives were busily establishing themselves in Canada, where unemployment was so chronic that very favourable wage settlements could be negotiated. However, some of the older generation were either in the UK or heading for it, and were bound to be in need of recommendations for financial advice.

The morning after their last meal, Bernard came breathlessly into the office and, without even stopping to pick up his phone messages, hurried into Malcolm's office and closed the door. "Problems, big problems," he announced. "Mr Chin must pay his deposit today by telegraphic transfer, and he can't. The bank is closed today. It's a public holiday on Jersey, the Battle of the Flowers or some such."

"Oh God," said Malcolm. "Can't he do it tomorrow before he leaves?

"No, he's got a six a.m. flight. I'm taking him to the airport myself," replied Bernard. "I can tell you, he isn't going to appreciate losing the house because the bank has a public holiday. The Chinese just don't understand that sort of thing."

"But surely it needn't come to that," said Malcolm. "All he has to do is call the solicitors and explain. They can verify the fact themselves if they want to."

Bernard smiled his man-of-the-world smile. "He wasn't the only interested party for that particular house and he did beat them down rather heavily. If there are any hitches, the vendor's solicitors are likely to recommend they try elsewhere. And it's not just that, it's the loss of face. If he had to break his word, he wouldn't be able to face going back to them again. You know what Orientals are like."

Malcolm didn't. In all his years in the Navy he'd been very careful not to find out. But he was prepared to take Bernard's word for it. Most of all, he didn't want to let Mr Chin out of their clutches.

Malcolm phoned through to Susie and ordered some coffee, while he pondered the problem in hand. Bernard remained silently puffing on an unlit cigar. Of course, there was only one solution: Malcolm and Bernard would have to provide the money, which they could lend to Mr Chin for a day or two at a suitably business-like rate. "Bringing good out of adversity," thought Malcolm, as Susie entered with two cups of cheap coffee dust. "How much have you got in the bank?" asked Malcolm.

"Virtually nothing just now," replied Bernard. "Marguerite took most of it to buy a chair lift for her mother and to pay for an extension for her house, so she doesn't need to keep going up and down stairs. It couldn't have come at a worse time; I've got money on deposit, but I can't get at it that quickly."

So that left Malcolm: he had some in the building society that he was going to use to part repay the loan on the yacht and he had some in the bank. He also had access to the office account at the bank. Together, there might just be enough. After several minutes' thought, he said, "Bernard, tell Mr Chin we know how to look after our clients here, and naturally we have no wish for him to be embarrassed, so I will personally provide the deposit money, from my own account."

"Are you sure?" asked Bernard. "It's a lot to ask, but I'm sure Mr Chin will be very grateful and would recompense you generously for your trouble and loss of interest, etc."

Malcolm was just calculating how big the "etc." should be, when Bernard broke in on his thoughts: "Only trouble is, it would have to be cash; Mr Chin would be terribly embarrassed offering a cheque from a third party."

"Look, Bernard, I'm perfectly willing to draw the cash from the bank and building society and hand it to you to hand to Mr Chin, on the understanding that you are responsible for its welfare: any losses, any problems with Mr Chin, will be down to you. It's your risk."

"I understand," replied Bernard gravely. "I'll write you a letter to that effect and have the girls in admin. witness my signature. I'll cover up the body of the letter so they won't know what it's about. When you've decided what to charge Mr Chin, I'll call him and tell him what we've arranged."

Malcolm ruminated on a plain digestive biscuit and settled for a modest 10% for two days' loan.

Bernard wrote his letter, which he duly deposited with Malcolm, and phoned Mr Chin. Mr Chin was inscrutably grateful and promised that the money plus the 10% consideration would be replaced by telegraphic transfer to Malcolm's account on the following day, when the request would be waiting at the Jersey bank as soon as it re-opened. Malcolm provided Bernard with his bank address and account number to pass on to Mr Chin, and the two of them set off to collect the cash. En route to the bank, Bernard said that after he had taken Mr Chin to the airport on the following day, he would go straight on to London to see a client, rather than back-track to the coast. He would call Malcolm during the afternoon to check that all was well and that he had got his money. Neither the bank nor the building society were particularly pleased to be relieved of so much money so early in the working day, and the bank even declared they would have to order up some more cash by special delivery truck, but somehow, together, they scraped up the £100,000. Bernard, remarking that he felt rather like a bank robber, drove off at speed for the marina, while Malcolm sauntered back to the office and the day's problems.

When he returned, Susie was gossiping to Ken and Colin, and they all turned to face him as he went past the door. He didn't like that: he could only hope Susie had the good sense to keep her mouth shut about his private arrangements with Bernard. She always had before, but now, he reflected, she was becoming increasingly friendly with Ken. "Have you lot earned so much this month that you can afford to hang about wasting time?" he asked loudly. The rest of the day crawled by. Business was slack and the reps. more pestilential than usual, with queries about regulations and complaints about shortages of forms. Malcolm didn't sleep well that night and insisted on getting himself and Susie into the office far earlier than usual on the following day.

He knew that Bernard had said he wouldn't be free to phone until after lunch with his client, but you never knew, he might just have a minute. But he didn't. Ken was in the outer office, making his usual round of phone calls, and once or twice he sat apparently studying Malcolm through the glass panels. Colin had managed to sell an endowment policy to support a mortgage the night before, and was gabbing on to Bill about how much more business he could get out of the young couple. Judging by the size of the mortgage, their joint income, and their heavy outgoings, Malcolm thought it would be a miracle if the mortgage-endowment lasted the year out. As he ate his luncheon meat sandwiches, Malcolm thought of Bernard entertaining his client and wondered when the lunch would end. Not until well after three, if it were up to Bernard's usual standard. Malcolm reflected that it seemed as if the whole office was waiting for something. He telephoned his bank. They declined to tell him the balance of his account over the phone. Stuff and nonsense regulations, not like the days when you knew your manager and he knew you. Nowadays Malcolm didn't really know who his bank manager was. Despite being kept annoyingly busy by phone calls from clients and office duties, Malcolm found the clock turning slowly through the hours until the banks, both on the mainland and on Jersey would be closed. Still no word from Bernard; he must have been held up.

At half past five, Malcolm could stand the tension no longer, so he phoned Bernard at home. No reply. There was nothing else to do but go home and try him in the evening. Marguerite was evidently still at her mother's, and Bernard appeared not to return home at all that evening. But still, there was not necessarily any cause for concern. Knowing Bernard, he'd probably taken his client clubbing and made a night of it. It was not unknown, but Malcolm was still on tenterhooks, and Susie seemed more than usually irritating, going on about the housekeeping and the fact that they couldn't really afford the boat.

After another sleepless night, Malcolm again dragged Susie into the office by 8.30. As the office started to fill up for the day's work, Malcolm sat drumming his fingers on his desk. Bill came in with a small medical insurance policy and, as Malcolm was distractedly checking the paperwork, he remarked brightly, "I bet you wish you'd gone out with Bernard and that Chinese guy on the boat now; it'll be lovely on the water."

Malcolm stopped dead. "What do you mean?"

"Oh, I saw Bernard and co. taking your boat out the day before yesterday, in the late morning when I was clearing up in the captain's cabin up at the marina. They'd had a bash the night before, and they asked me to lend them a hand."

"Did they say where they were going?" asked Malcolm, trying to keep the panic out of his voice.

"I didn't see them to talk to, you know. I only saw them out of the window. Is that OK about him having appendicitis complications, do you think?"

"Oh, I'm sure it's fine," replied Malcolm absently. He signed the paperwork off and hustled Bill out of the office.

With a shaking hand, he dialled the number of the bank in Jersey, which would now be open. He had friends there; they would help him. They didn't, except to inform him that Mr Chin had withdrawn all his money, in person, the day before the holiday. He'd flown over for the day for the purpose. No, they didn't know where he was planning to go after that. Malcolm just about saved himself from being sick. No sooner had he replaced the receiver, than the phone rang. It was a hysterical Marguerite, calling from her mother's. She'd just received a second class letter from Bernard. He'd left her and, during her absence, had sold their house and furniture and taken all the money with him. She wouldn't see him again. Perhaps in the future her mother would support her taste in clothes and antiques. Malcolm clapped his hand over his mouth. He removed it to tell Marguerite he didn't know what had become of Bernard. He hadn't given notice at the office. He'd last been seen in the company of a Mr Chin. Had Marguerite any idea where they might head for? "Mr Chin?" exploded Marguerite at the other end of the line. "You mean that awful man who used to be Bernard's sergeant in the Hong Kong police? The one who used to take bribes."

That at least explained Mr Chin's affluence. Malcolm dropped the receiver and ran to the Gents.

After about fifteen minutes, he'd regained his physical composure. The thing to do was to go back to the office and take stock of the situation. Save face in front of the troops. He sauntered casually back to his room. He sat down before he fainted. He'd lost £100,000 and, worse yet, he'd lost the yacht. Bernard and Mr Chin had conned him rotten. Realistically speaking, he had no hope of getting them back. Bernard was nothing if not a planner. By now Malcolm's boat would be in some shady continental boat yard, being re-painted, re-named and re-provenanced. After that, with his money and the money from the sale of Bernard's house and possessions, the world was their oyster. Malcolm was afraid to call the police: he'd stolen money from the office account to give to Bernard. Above all, he had to get that replaced before they found out. Conned by two ex-cops on a spree. Oh God. Without Bernard's arrangement Malcolm knew he would never earn enough money every month to keep the mortgage and the bank loan for the yacht going. He was bust all over again. He'd have to sell the house sharpish to repay the stolen money into the office account. How could he have been such a fool?

His speculations were interrupted by Ken and Susie coming into his office. Susie looked like a guilty schoolgirl, but Ken was more self-possessed. He sat down and came straight to the point. "No Bernard this morning then?"

"Eh? No. Bernard may not be with us much longer," replied Malcolm cautiously.

Ken smiled his lovely smile. "Funny bloke Bernard; had a chap like him in my sales office in the States. Tried to bribe me to give him all the good dealerships, so he could make all the fleet sales and get more commission. Turned him down flat of course. Very dangerous thing to do. Instant dismissal if found out…" He paused.

Susie had obviously talked. "Don't look at me like that, Malcolm," she said crossly, the colour rising on her face and throat. "It was obvious to anyone with eyes what was going on. Ken's not a fool you know. In fact… well, I, we… well I tried to tell you last night, but you were so irritable. Truth is, Malcolm, I know this isn't the time or place, but I'm fed up. I've had enough. Ken and I, well, we like one another. Very much, and… well, I'm sorry, Malcolm, but it's over."

"Don't take it too hard." Ken clapped Malcolm on the arm. "It's better than both being unhappy together, and you'll pick up, bounce back. You did before, and you'll hardly miss the £1,000 a month."

"So that was it," thought Malcolm. "Simple blackmail and a shared taste for Earl Grey." Malcolm shrugged in Susie's direction. "If it's what you want."

"It is," she said simply. Ken and Susie left the office together, closing the door quietly behind them. It never rained but what it poured. Malcolm knew that Ken would see to it that Susie got half the value of the house when he sold.

Colin entered. "Bernard's gone then." Colin was always one for stating the obvious.

"Apparently, yes," replied Malcolm tersely. The last thing he wanted now was Colin.

"So what I thought," prattled Colin, "With me being your number two earner, I should take over his clients and, of course, all those leads he used to get. He won't need them now."

"Over my dead body," thought Malcolm. He said, "More like than not, I shall take them over myself."

"I'd be very grateful," said Colin, through his toothy smile. "About twenty per cent grateful. That's about right isn't it?"

Malcolm was very close to a heart attack. This really was the end. Colin would never be able to sell to the sort of clients Bernard had had. The workhouse was staring him in the face, but he couldn't risk antagonizing Colin. He couldn't risk him ratting to head office. His dry throat uttered, "Yes, that's about it."

At least Colin knew when he wasn't wanted. He pulled on his red braces, sprang up, and left Malcolm's office with a parting shot: "It's not that bad, Malcolm; I'm not asking much, and as they say: 'Greed is good'."

It may be, but, as Bernard and Mr Chin were soon to find out in their Mediterranean haven, religion is more profitable.

SHIMMERING SHORES

By about half past four Jack was driving over the brow of the hill on the A road as it reached the town centre. Spread below he could see Stevens Gardens, with the heavy Victorian fountain splashing its spray in the breeze. Tourists were laid out next to the flower beds and the coach park was alive with early afternoon departures. According to his map The Albion Hotel was directly on the seafront behind the gardens. As he crawled along in the traffic his eyes scanned for a sign, but the Albion was obviously one of those establishments which did not care to – or better yet – did not need to indulge in garish advertisement.

As he viewed the calm bay he was struck by what appeared to be a mirage. Common sense told him that those houses and that church could not be growing out of the sea.

The traffic surged forward and he anxiously sought out his hotel. When he looked round again the island was still glittering in the summer sun, but his hotel was not. Having twice gone round the huge roundabout surrounding Stevens Gardens, he cursed Henry. Why send him a map if it was not accurate?

Seizing his opportunity, Jack parked in the YMCA car park and nipped out to ask directions.

The stubbly receptionist looked at him with a mixture of mirth and suspicion. "The Albion Hotel? Wot? You some kind of joker or something?"

"No, I'm not a joker. I'm a very tired visitor. It's taken me five hours in the baking heat to get here, and now that I am here, all I want to do is find my hotel. If you don't know where it is, just say so."

"Keep your shirt on. The Albion used to be over there, behind the war memorial, but it won't do you any good."

Jack turned sharply, grabbed his grip out of the car and cut across the gardens.

No hotel. There was, however, a resort directory. Under the hotel listings, Jack sought in vain for the Albion. He called Henry at his office. Henry was in a meeting and had indicated that he did not wish to be disturbed. Jack asked his PA for directions to the hotel.

"Where are you now Mr Tranter?"

"By the war memorial. I'm standing in front of the directory boards."

The PA sounded puzzled: "Then you can't miss it. It's the white stucco building, the one with the two columns by the main entrance. I'm sure you'll find it very comfortable."

Jack looked around. No white stucco. No columns. This town was obviously peopled by the insane. He marched back to his car and returned his grip. The smell of the flowers and the laughter of the youngsters cheered him a little. This was probably Henry's idea of a joke. They would have a laugh about it tomorrow. There was no reason to let this bit of silliness spoil the evening. He decided to wander over to the seafront and look out for a B and B. Seaside towns were always knee-deep in these excellent little residences. Finding accommodation, even in the high season, would present no problem. But Henry would have to pay – oh yes – it would be five star lunches and dinners for the next two days.

When he reached the seafront, Jack was drawn towards the ornate pier, gay with its lights and restaurants, but thought it advisable to seek out a quieter quarter for a good night's rest. As he turned, he saw the island again: solid bricks and mortar rising out of the bay. It must be a new development, architecturally, it certainly looked modern. How had they got that past the Environment Authority?

As far as Jack could tell, the only approach to the island lay across the beach. Gingerly, he picked his way past the air beds and food baskets. No one paid him any heed. Perhaps he could find a guest house on the island.

As he drew near Jack noticed that, apart from the church, all the buildings appeared to be shops with accommodation on the upper floors. He could see why: the sea was lapping at the low shingle bank which surrounded the island. It would not take much for the water to over-top it and flood the lower storeys. Presumably the residents preferred losing their stock to losing their belongings. Now there was a causeway, built out of the skeletons of long-dead crustaceans, stones, and a lip-service of cement. He cursed as the tide washed his brogues.

The causeway led to the right-hand corner of the island and gave way directly into a cobbled square. The artificial square was a-buzz with tourists hunting through the classy souvenir shop and the local artists' gallery. Jack was tempted to buy a sea-view, but he decided to look round first.

He re-traced his way out of the square and walked along the paved path which gave a view of the shore and fronted the olde-worlde twenty-first century tearooms and bakery. Edna's establishment looked and smelt tempting, and Jack was hungry. As he entered, the door rang an old-fashioned brass bell, and a waitress dressed in a long black gown, a white apron and cap came out to serve him. Having placed his order, Jack enquired about lodgings for the night.

His waitress was doubtful: "I don't think there is anywhere at all on the island, sir. We don't do rooms and the pub only has a couple upstairs, and they're usually taken."

The Earl Grey and real cream cakes were delicious. Slipping a substantial cash tip under his saucer, Jack proffered his credit card for the bill. His waitress stared at it and blushed. "That's OK, isn't it? Or don't you take them?"

"Oh yes, sir. Yes indeed, Mr Tranter." The waitress took his card and conversed with an older lady housed behind an antique metal till. They both scrutinized Jack before completing his transaction.

Strolling further along the paved way, Jack came to another side path, the equivalent of that leading from the causeway, which housed a single, very elegant, boutique. He whistled when he saw the prices attached to the skimpy, limp dresses. The folk who lived here might not be secure against the forces of nature, but they knew how to make a buck. A smartly dressed woman exited and brushed silently past him. He followed her back into the square, coming out by the side of the church. It was a striking structure, well built and sturdy, with modern abstract stained glass windows. Its spire rose well above the other buildings on the island and it looked curiously out of place amongst the shops.

Jack espied the pub directly across the square. There would be no harm in asking. Like Edna's Tearooms, it aped the Victorian era, but looked welcoming enough. Jack noted the omission of outside tables and benches, but surmised that the square was too small to permit the hostelry to spill its customers across the shop fronts. As it swayed in the freshening breeze, the wooden sign creaked in its ornate metal frame, and Jack had to bend his head to read it. No wonder the waitress had regarded him with interest.

He pushed open the swing doors into the single bar, which was full, but not over-crowded. "Pint of Webster's please."

The barman, stolid in his white shirt and arm-bands, stared before replying. "Webster's? I'm afraid we don't have that, sir. We've got Jacob's or Murray's or Golden Tankard."

Jack was puzzled; he had never heard of any of these. Presumably, they were local beers, bought in to encourage the drinkers to enter the olde-worlde spirit. "What would you recommend?"

"Why not try the Murray's, sir? That's always very popular."

"The waitress in the tearooms said that you have a couple of rooms here. I'm looking for a place for tonight; my hotel has let me down."

"That's a shame, sir, but I'm afraid we can't help you. We're full."

Jack probed his pint. "Your pub has a very unusual name; 'Tranter's Folly'."

The barman appeared not to find it strange. "That's not surprising, is it, sir? All things considered. This is Tranter's Island, after all."

Jack drank a mouthful. It tasted as though sea water had got into the barrel. "I didn't know that. But why 'Folly'?"

The barman laughed. "It stands to reason. That's what this whole place is, from start to finish. It was a daft idea. Pattie and me, we're fine. We do well enough here and we didn't have to put any of our own money down to get the tenancy. We rent it from a management company, and they were only too glad to get someone to take it on. The vicar's the same."

Jack abandoned his beer. "I don't understand."

"Well, his management put him in too. He doesn't have to pay rent or spend any of his own money on his place, unlike the other poor devils here. I don't know how some of them manage. The tearooms aren't so bad, there's always a good seasonal trade; but that dress shop and the butcher. I ask you, friend, a butcher for less than twenty families. Where's the sense in that?"

"I see your point, but I thought there looked to be a good deal of money about in the square just now."

"Yeh, but none of it lives here. Come the early evening, they're off back to their hotels, like you would be if you had one. We're the only ones what get anything later."

Jack could restrain his professional curiosity no longer. "Your island is certainly a fascinating place. I'm a civil engineer and I was wondering how the developers got permission to build it here in the bay."

"Ah, well." The barman tapped the side of his nose. "There's a few would like to know the answer to that one. After all, there's no point in them suing the builders, is there? Not when they're bust and dead, in that order. Now, if they could prove that the Environment lot or the City Development Partnership were at fault, they might stand some chance of getting their money back, even after all these years."

"And the residents would want that? To leave here?"

"Are you joking, friend? Wouldn't you, if your place was flooded every spring tide? But they're stuck; they can't sell and now they can't even claim off insurances. They stopped getting cover years ago."

"I did wonder. The retaining wall around the island looked very low to me."

"It wouldn't make any difference. When the rollers come in off the North Sea, nothing stops them. The place is swamped. Luckily, it's mostly out of season."

Jack thought that little story would do much to explain the quality of his beer. For the sake of politeness he tried again.

"That's where me and the vicar scores again, see. We're both higher up than the other places, so we don't usually get it, except in the cellar. The rest of them know when to expect it, and they take most of their stock and fittings upstairs, and hope for the best. Mind you, me and Pattie don't do too bad out of it. The folk from them little souvenir shops haven't got much room upstairs, so they has to lodge with us, and what we make out of them covers any costs we might get. The vicar helps out too, of course, showing the proper Christian attitude and all that. But I wish he wouldn't undercut the room rate."

Jack almost choked. "Well, thanks for the beer; it's been very interesting talking to you, but I'd better be off in search of a room."

"There's a couple of side streets west of the pier with a few good commercial hotels and the like. You could do worse than try one of those."

Jack thanked the barman and returned to the square. It was later than he had thought and most of the tourists had departed.

Voices floated from outside a minute general store and post office on the seaward side of the square. "You bring the news-board in, Jack, and I'll finish round the side."

Jack wandered over to where a middle-aged couple were closing up for the day. The man was wearing check trousers and a pale yellow golfing sweater and the woman was dressed in floral print. She was sweeping the cobbles with a besom.

Jack inspected the shop front. Above the door was the official line: "Post Office. J.M. Tranter." J.M. Jack? "Excuse me, Mr Tranter, is it?"

"Yes. Can I help you? We're just closing."

"I don't want to buy anything, thank you, but I couldn't help noticing your wife called you 'Jack'. So you are Jack Tranter?"

"Yes. Why do you ask?"

"So am I."

The woman returned from her sweeping and scrutinized the new Jack. "Do you come from these parts, then?"

"No. I'm visiting for a few days and when I saw this little island, I thought I would explore. Then I found out it was called Tranter's Island, and now I find you, sharing my name."

"It was our father who built the island, Edna is my sister. We were named for our parents."

"So this development was your father's idea?"

"Him and his business partner, Henry Curtiss. Do you know the story?"

Jack was startled. "That name rings a bell. What happened?"

Edna was suspicious, but her brother was only too ready to tell the tale. "Tranter's were a firm of civil engineers, and Curtiss' were the architects. In those days, everyone wanted a place by the sea. Marinas and retirement villages were all the thing. They thought they would go one better and build themselves an island. Least ways, there were a couple of small natural islands here already. The church now stands on one and the pub on the other. They did like the Dutch do: they built a wall and drained the intervening space. The rest of the buildings here are built on piles, like in Venice."

"There was a lot of local opposition: the residents and hoteliers along the front didn't like it because it spoiled the coastal views."

"What about the planners?" asked Jack. "I would have thought something as striking as this would have been difficult to get permission for."

Edna replied in a tone bitterly at odds with the beauty of the time and place: "You may well ask. That's something we'd all like to know. Rumour has it that Curtiss bribed both the chairman of the City Development Partnership and the local Environment Officer, but we've never been able to prove it. If we could prove mal-administration, we could sue and get off this island."

"I'm sorry it's turned out so badly for you. The landlord of the pub did tell me you get flooded quite often."

"Cyril? He's all right. He's got money. None of us has," replied Jack. "We're worse off than most. Our father went bankrupt over this place, so we've never had a bean. The two lots he bought here are all we've ever had, and we only managed to keep them because they were in our mother's name."

Edna fingered her gold locket. “As it is this place isn’t worth anything at all. My daughter Angela has to work in the tearooms.”

Jack struggled to find words to comfort the bitter couple. “Surely though, your father did no wrong. He would never have bought property here if he had believed there was anything fundamentally wrong with the project. If Henry Curtiss did offer bribes, he must have kept it from him. What happened to Curtiss, by the way?”

“He died shortly after the island was completed. There was a civic bash in the old Albion Hotel to celebrate the opening. Fortunately, our parents didn’t attend. Someone got careless in the kitchens and the whole place went up like a torch. He’s buried over in the church, near dad. He died of a heart attack twenty years ago come August.”

Jack knew the answer before he asked the question: “And I suppose they never rebuilt the hotel?”

No, there’s just a memorial plaque there now. It used to stand by Stevens Gardens.”

Jack noticed a bucket containing bunches of flowers parked by the door. He picked a posy of summer flowers. “I know you’re closed, but will a tenner do? Then I’d better let you get on.”

“Fine, if you’re sure. Thank you very much. Take care, now.”

Neither of them noticed Jack make his way across the square to the church. It proved to be well built and well maintained. Beautifully manicured brickwork surrounded the archway, and the door was open. The builders must have used a salt-resistant mortar. It did not take him long to find the plaque. It was a few feet away from that of Henry Curtiss and was surrounded by others, bearing unfamiliar names. Deceased islanders were presumably cremated and commemorated by these plaques because the island lacked a proper graveyard.

There was no memory of an Edna Tranter. Finding no vase, Jack undid his bundle and placed the flowers individually in the aisle beneath the wall. He stood back and was silent for several minutes before saying: “Not this time. There will be no island.

No Tranter's Folly."

A female voice behind him asked, "But then what will become of us, Jack? This is our island, there is no other place for us." It was the proprietress from the tearooms. Her face was softly radiant in the dancing spectrum.

Jack smiled at the sound of her voice.

"If Tranter's Island never exists, then those born here, our children and grandchildren, will have no place in the world."

"I've met our children over at the Post Office. All I gave them and the others was a life of misery."

"You gave them my darling Angela. Happiness is not within your power or mine to give, Jack. Be content to ensure that the development is properly constructed and safe to live in. The future is a closed book; even though you have been given the chance to re-write some of the pages, you cannot ensure a happy ending."

He kissed Edna lightly on the forehead. "I'll watch Henry Curtiss like a hawk."

Edna smiled. "That's my Jack."

Holding both her hands, he asked: "Tell me, when do I get to meet you?"

"Go back now. They serve dinner early at The Albion. I'm sure you will enjoy your stay."

THE BLUE JAGUAR

There was no doubt about it, Alina was becoming an expense: very beautiful, but non-tax-deductible. Richard hadn't expected that of course when he had married her five years ago. Quite the reverse in fact. After all, she'd hardly been used to the finer things in life. As a school teacher in Warsaw very few of the finer things had been available to her, which was how they had come to meet. She'd been working nights as a hostess in a club, and Richard had met her on one of his business trips. They'd become friendly and, Richard being recently divorced, one thing had led to another. As he sat at the old pine table which served as his working desk when he was at home and looked out on the sodden leaves in the back garden, her voice came back to him. "Even the lavatory cleaners at the airport make more than I do. Tips, you know, from foreigners." His laughter echoed in his brain and he remembered the size of the tip he'd left her that evening. Not so much a tip really, more a down-payment.

"It's only right, after all, Richard and you promised." She was off again. Nagging about a private school for young Dominic, their four-year-old son.

"I know I did, but I simply can't afford it. Not now. Business is lousy. Well you know that, you read the papers. And besides, he doesn't have to go to school yet. There's no need to panic."

"I am not panicking, as you put it, I just want to make sure we have enough to send him to a good school. Have you seen how much even the day schools cost?" He looked over his shoulder and saw her waving a bunch of brochures at him. "And besides, if you're paying for Dick and Robert, you can afford to pay for Nicky."

"That's different, they were already at school when Hazel and I divorced. It was part of the settlement that I went on paying for them. Besides, it would be wrong to move them now they're coming up to exams." He knew the minute he'd finished speaking that he'd said the wrong thing.

"You shouldn't make such settlements with your old wife if you cannot do the same for your new one. You should go and get it changed. She's bleeding you dry. Look at the way we have to live." It was the old story. Ever since they'd married and she'd discovered the terms of the divorce settlement, Alina had been gunning for Hazel, and, in truth, there was some justice in her claim. Hazel and her daddy had stitched him up good and proper. She'd got the house, a very generous allowance and private education for the boys. Daddy had been very definite on that point; the education, and the contacts and finesse which St. Bartholomew's private academy provided were indispensable for any young gentleman. Richard thought it most curious that with all his inherited wealth daddy had never felt it incumbent on himself to assist with the payments for such a necessity for his grandchildren.

"You're not even listening to me," she screeched. It was true. He wasn't. He didn't need to: he could sing along with her arguments, he'd heard them so often before. "Look at this house. A four-bedroom box on a housing estate. It's not suitable for people in our position."

"You liked it well enough when you badgered me into buying it," he countered.

"It was all we could afford. It was the best of a bad bunch."

"We could afford? We? Who's we?" he shouted angrily. "I never noticed that you brought in anything much in the way of money."

"At least I was honest with you," she snapped. "But you… you…" She waved her arms about in rage and frustration. "You and your big talk about building houses and owning restaurants. How many houses have you built since we were married? Go on: just tell me. Business is lousy you say. You always say that. For you it always is. You never get off your backside and do any work."

"That's it," he yelled. "I'm off out, and if you think I'm going to waste good money sending that brat…"

The door bell rang. Alina answered it. On the step she saw a middle-aged woman in an ancient tweed suit. "Good morning, Alice Winthrop from Shore Brothers, for Mr Bishop."

"Oh God," muttered Richard. He'd completely forgotten the appointment he'd made with the financial adviser. Alina admitted her with ill-concealed annoyance and, scooping up Nicky, flounced upstairs with him, leaving Richard to cope unaided. Mrs Winthrop looked around her as Richard dragged up an extra chair and cleared a space on the table. This would just suit Alina, of course. It was she who'd nagged him into promising to set up a saving scheme for Nicky in the first place. Well, if she thought he was going ahead with that after this morning's show, she was mistaken. The thing to do was to let this silly old cow make her notes and ask her questions and then get rid of her. That would keep the peace a bit. At least Alina couldn't say he hadn't tried. Richard was used to dealing with financial advisers; business attracted them like flies. They were all the same. Except this one, who seemed to be more inept than usual.

Still, he plodded on through the endless stupid questions on the planning questionnaire, and Mrs Winthrop duly and seriously noted the answers. She appeared to have no idea how a businessman operated and, as she nervously shuffled her pages, Richard thought it looked like this was her first week in the job. And likely to be her last is she didn't buck up. "I've worked hard all my life," he said. "After my father died and left me that half million, I invested it in the best way of all. In myself. I've worked my way up with the building business and the restaurant I own. The Olde Oake Barn. Just across from your offices. I expect you know it. Well you can see for yourself how well we live." Just then a car drew up outside their front windows. Richard bounded across the through lounge and opened the front window. "Why can't you park that thing in front of your own house?" he yelled at the occupant, who was struggling to extricate himself from the driver's seat.

"You don't own the road, Richard. It's not doing any harm." The driver went into the house next door.

Richard slammed the window shut and returned to Mrs

Winthrop, who kindly offered, "Yes, that's the trouble with housing estates. Too close together. You're only as good as your neighbours." Richard wondered what sort of dump she lived in. He sat impatiently while Mrs Winthrop tapped away at her calculator. She concluded, "So you're a very busy man. I can see that." She smiled hopefully. Richard yawned. "Well I think that looks like, with the business expenses over the years and all that, you've got net assets of about a quarter of a million, altogether." She beamed, as if she expected Richard to be pleased. He wasn't. He was angry. Mrs Winthrop, with a singular lack of tact, had just pointed out to him that all his years' work had simply resulted in him losing a quarter of a million.

The door bell rang again. "Excuse me," said Richard abruptly. He knew full well that Alina wasn't going to condescend to answer it. As Mrs Winthrop looked speculatively around the untidy living room, her gaze travelled to the front of the room and, parked behind the neighbour's offending vehicle, she could just make out the bonnet of a dark blue Jaguar. The conversation from the front door drifted towards her. "So Mr Bishop, Mr Sopwith asked me to deliver the car personally. All the documentation is here, and your complimentary champagne, of course. I hope you enjoy driving her. She's a beauty."

"Thank you," said Richard tersely, and closed the door on the car salesman's nose. Another complication. He'd asked Sopwith's if they could keep the car in the showroom until he'd cleared out the double garage and made room to put it in. Considering the price of the vehicle, it wasn't much to ask, but oh no, having made the sale, Sopwith's had decided they didn't have room either and, after merely seven days, had delivered the Jag to his home. Now he'd have to spend the rest of the morning carting the junk from the garage to the works to get rid of it. Either that or the idiot next door would reverse into his new car.

"Lovely car you've got there," said Mrs Winthrop brightly, as Richard returned. "Look, is this it then?" he asked crossly. "I mean, you've got all the details, haven't you? You know what I want, so produce some quotations for me and I'll think them over."

"Well," said Mrs Winthrop uncertainly, "I did just think, one thing strikes me immediately, if you know what I mean." Richard folded his arms and stood over her.

"Yes," he said sharply.

"Well," she continued, "With you being so busy, have you ever wondered what would happen if… Alina… your wife wasn't here any more?" Little did she know, that thought had crossed Richard's mind quite a lot in the past few weeks. He smiled grimly. Mrs Winthrop ploughed on gamely, "I know it's not a pleasant subject, but as a practical man, you're sensible enough to realize that talking about it doesn't bring it any closer and, after all, it's best to make provision for these things before they happen."

"Get on with it," cut in Richard impatiently.

She paused and took a deep breath. "After all, who'd look after little Dominic? You'd have to hire a housekeeper. And, believe me, they don't come cheap. So what you should do, is to take out some insurance on Alina. It needn't cost very much if she's in good health and it would be peace of mind." She looked up at him hopefully.

"Look, as you can see, I'm very busy, so why don't you make your recommendations in writing and post them to me?" He offered his hand as if to shake hers, indicating that the interview was over, and practically threw her out of the house. On her way down the drive Mrs Winthrop found time to pause and admire the car more closely. He'd even got a personalized number plate.

When he'd finally got rid of her, Richard went into the kitchen to brew himself a cup of instant coffee before tackling the garage. Little did she know, he would be only too glad if Alina were to suddenly die and disappear from his life, and as for Nicky: that boy was the spitting image of his mother: grab, grab, grab. It would be a pleasure to let him loose on an unsuspecting social services department. As he downed the dregs of his coffee, he wondered how long Mrs Winthrop would last in business; what with her lack of tact and stupid ideas, he didn't think it would be long. Surely, even she could see that he couldn't afford any extra outlay at present, least of all on life assurance. What a waste. He went out the back door and into the garage.

As he was heaving timber into the back of the firm's Land Rover, Richard could see Alina and Nicky at the bottom of the drive. Alina was stroking the bonnet of the Jaguar and chatting to June from next door.

"It's beautiful," said June. "Wish we could afford one."

"So do I," muttered Richard under his breath.

Alina seemed to grow taller by about three inches. "Oh well, you know Richard's doing very well."

"He must be the only builder who is," said June cheerfully. "Nothing but doom and gloom if you look at the news. Still, if you can do it, there must be work out there somewhere."

"Oh yes, we have no problems like that," replied Alina complacently. "We were thinking of moving a while back. You know, get a plot and build our own house in the country, but Richard's so cautious. Typical man," she laughed.

Richard was rapidly coming to the conclusion that Alina was living in a different world to the one he inhabited. They'd never discussed moving. There was no point. He could barely pay the mortgage on the place they'd got. There hadn't been a decent contract for months. They were just ticking over, doing odd jobs here and there. Alina knew full well he'd had to lay off about sixty per cent of his staff. And now he had this bloody car to pay for. But she was a beauty, and he'd wanted a new car, especially a Jaguar.

"Oh well, mustn't stand here all day," said June and she walked away up her own driveway. Alina walked back to the garage with Dominic behind her.

"She's beautiful Richard; we must go out for lunch. Give her a spin."

"Not today," he replied bluntly. "I've got too much work to do." But he was, nevertheless, very proud. She was definitely a car to be noticed.

When he got to the yard with the timber, he got a couple of the trainees to offload it while he went into the office. Gladys was on the phone with the diary open in front of her. He glanced down: a couple of requests for estimates. Nothing big. She put the phone down. "Not too good I'm afraid, Mr Bishop."

"I can see that for myself," he said and then stomped off. Looking round the yard he remembered what it had been like when his father was alive: busy, full of compliant cheerful, cheap craftsmen. There had always been plenty of work then. They'd had to turn it away. And with the work had come the lifestyle: a farmhouse with ponies for the children, a Rover and a motorcruiser. Now what had he got? A handful of grumbling, overpaid, underworked, spotty youths, no boat, no ponies and definitely no farmhouse. Ah well; he'd got the car. Just about.

Richard's real problem was that he liked the lifestyle of a rich man, the luxury and the leisure, but he hadn't the energy and acumen to support it. After his father had died unexpectedly at the age of fifty-nine, the business had simply gone straight downhill and expenditure straight uphill. As he drove slowly home Richard considered his position. It was simply not right that someone of his importance should not be able to enjoy life. Penny-pinching and nine-to-five were for poor people. That's how they got by. But he didn't want to get by. He wanted to be able to do what he wanted when he wanted, and he simply had to admit he couldn't do that with Alina. She was turning into an encumbrance. Rapidly. God knew why. With her background she should be grateful enough for what she'd got, not always demanding, nagging. It wasn't that Richard objected to spending money; he didn't. But he wanted to spend it his way: a good house, certainly, a couple of servants, a boat, and endless rounds down the club. What he did not want was to spend it on tacky furniture, package holidays and private schools for the kids. He'd never had a private education and he was none the worse for it. He was a businessman, a self-made man and proud of it. Never mind what that stupid woman Winthrop had said. She didn't understand business. Women never did; they simply couldn't understand it was necessary to borrow to expand.

Just before he reached their executive exclusive housing estate, he pulled the Land Rover into a lay-by and watched the leaves falling from the trees. Winter would be on him before he knew it. He sat, reflecting, surrounded by the smoke from his cigarette. He'd go on paying for the two oldest boys until they left school, and not a moment longer. If they wanted to go to college, Hazel's dear daddy could pay for them, or they could get jobs part-time like other students had to. After all, he'd started working the minute he'd left school; there was no reason why they shouldn't do the same. Hazel herself was a problem he was stuck with. There was no way out of that except to go back to court for a variation of the order. He thought about it, but all that would do was shove more money the way of his lawyers, and there was a good chance that even then he'd still come out a loser. He lit another cigarette and considered Alina. Divorce was the obvious solution. With a bit of luck, he could get her and the boy bundled off back to Poland, so that she could be near her family, God help them. It was a funny thing, but he'd never taken to Nicky; the boy was so like his mother and nothing like him. Greedy. That was the problem: Alina was greedy, but she wasn't stupid. She'd never settle for less than Hazel had got, and she'd never go back to Poland. There simply wasn't enough money in the whole of that country to satisfy her. Richard groaned; he couldn't afford to divorce her, and he couldn't stand living with her. He could see it all stretching before him: the years of rows and demands. In ten years' time she wouldn't even be attractive, already now the lines were beginning to form around her eyes and mouth. The wind picked up and cast a few more leaves on to the dampness of the lane. What a depressing prospect.

Richard just couldn't face going home. He wanted to drive out of the lay-by and drive forever, past the housing estate, on to the motorway, on to the ferry to France, and away. To drive forever and never arrive. To leave it all behind. It was then that it occurred to him that if he couldn't leave everything behind him, Alina could. Permanently. As he thought about it, the idea became more and more attractive. A beautiful sun on an autumn day. And, yes, there was a bonus. It could even become a paying prospect. What had that Mrs Winthrop said about insuring his wife in case anything happened to her? What a good idea. Of course he wouldn't use the money to get a housekeeper to look after the boy; he'd dump him on the state. A lone father couldn't possibly be expected to cope with that little horror. With any luck he might even have enough to pay off Hazel in a lump sum and get rid of her for ever. Richard threw the Land Rover into gear and drove off towards a bright new future.

In the days that followed he haunted the postbox in the mornings, waiting for the quotations from Mrs Winthrop to arrive. He'd managed to pacify Alina by promising to do something about Dominic's schooling and had even got into her good books by mentioning his plan to insure her life. "Just to protect the lad's interests in case the worst happens. You never know. After all, I'm insured. It's only right you should be too. And it won't cost much." It certainly wouldn't. Not for the length of time he was anticipating paying the premiums. When the quotations arrived, Richard duly pondered over them and picked a reasonable looking amount: not too much. It mustn't look suspicious. Within half a day he'd got Alina to agree and had called Mrs Winthrop.

When Mrs Winthrop received his phone call summoning her to the house to effect £50,000 insurance for Alina, she thought it was Christmas come early. Privately, she'd set Richard down as an arrogant prat who would never learn to do what was in his own best interests. But, she cheerfully admitted to herself, she was as capable of being wrong as the next person. And so it was that, meticulously attired and equipped with spare copies of all the application and medical forms, she set off for a good day's work. And it was all so easy: Richard was keen to get on with it and, after an initial bit of feminine hostility, marked by the asking of numerous petty and irrelevant questions, Alina was happy enough to complete the paperwork. "Mind you," thought Mrs Winthrop on the way back to her car, "that child is a terror. I'm glad I don't have to bring him up. I wonder where he gets it from?"

Autumn became winter, which in turn greened into spring,

as Richard struggled on, making the payments on his mortgage, bank loans, credit cards and insurance policies. Sometimes his bank refused to oblige him. He'd put the actual deed of murder from his mind over Christmas, telling himself that it would be foolish to act too soon. And there was always the possibility of a genuine accident. But no such luck. Come March Alina was still there, as demanding as ever, and not looking as though she might ever get ill at all. She had not even had a cold all winter. It was no good. He would have to do the deed himself. And so it was that Richard took to browsing the true crime section of the local library, watching TV documentaries on crime and even, on occasion, Crimewatch. The problem with all these sources of information, however, was that they were, by definition, failed crimes. The perpetrators had been caught. Richard most definitely did not want to emulate them in that respect. What he needed was something simple, something believable and, preferably, something cheap.

The idea finally came to him on one of his regular inspection visits to the Olde Oake Barn. He didn't really know why he had hung on to the bar/restaurant. It was more trouble than it was worth. It was a good half hour's drive from home, and he never enjoyed the journey along the crowded coast road. Stuck in the usual traffic jam approaching the town centre, he reflected, not for the first time, on what a chancy affair running a restaurant was. Here were all these motorists crawling nose to bumper only a couple of streets away from his eatery. And yet none of them ever seemed to stop in the town, get out of their cars and walk through his front doors. The few other hostelries on that windswept portion of the Channel coast seemed to do fairly well, but his was always suspiciously empty. And it wasn't that he hadn't tried. He'd modernised the exterior and completely redecorated the interior in the olde-worlde smuggling style he thought appropriate for these marshes. And managers: he'd had enough of those to last him a lifetime. Perhaps he should get rid of these two and try again. But then again, every new couple seemed worse than the last.

He managed to get to his turning off the main road and drove past Shore Brothers up the comparatively narrow road approaching the Barn. It was as he expected: the car park was empty even though it was well into the morning opening time. The yard didn't look as though it had been swept in a week. It gave a bad impression. He would have to talk to Mac about it, after he had been through the books. Parking his Jaguar by some empty barrels at the rear of the bar, he let himself in the back door, using his spare keys. The back door led directly to Mac and Janice's private quarters and, without bothering to greet them, Richard made his way into Mac's office-living room and picked up the ledgers, which were kept on the desk. As he read through the pages he swore softly to himself. It went from bad to worse. No doubt about it, they would have to go.

When he'd seen enough Richard left the office and started to go forward towards the bar. Then he saw Mac emerging from the cellar. "What the hell are you doing pussyfooting around here, Richard?" he asked crossly.

"Looking at the books."

Mac came out of the cellar and, leaving the stair door open, rounded on Richard. "Look, I've told you before about that. This is our home. Our private home. If you want to come in and look over the books or anything else, ask, like everyone else has to."

Richard started forward. "Look matey, I own this place. Not you. Me. Got that? If I want to come in here, I will, any time I like. And there's nothing you can do about it. And a bloody good job I did too. What the hell have you two been up to this last quarter? This is a business you know, not an alms house, not a charity."

Mac rolled his eyes upward. "Here we go again. I've told you before, if you won't have the place done up properly and won't let me stock what the punters want, you can't expect them to come in. It's as simple as that. Your trouble, Richard, is that you're a meddler; you don't want to do the job yourself, but you won't let me and Janice get on with it either. You want to make your mind up about what you want."

He turned and went into the bar. Richard started to follow him and almost fell down the cellar steps. He was about to cry out, but something stopped him, and he stepped back and pulled the door shut. That was it. So simple. So obvious. A fall down the cellar steps when an incompetent barman had left the door open and that was it. No more Alina. Richard called after Mac, "I'm off now, but don't think you've heard the last of this." He slammed out through the apartment and back to his own car. He sat in the deserted yard thinking things over. Of course it would need careful handling, but he was in no doubt that a good hard shove down those steps would do the job. All the way home he was planning how it should be done. He even considered increasing Alina's insurance, but decided against it on the grounds that it would look too suspicious. Unlike his dear wife, he wasn't going to let greed trap him into folly.

The next month slipped by without any major upsets, until it was time to make another inspection visit to the Barn. By the time the day came, Richard had even decided that after the tragedy, he would sell the place. It would only be natural. He could hardly be expected to keep the place running after his poor wife had met her untimely death in the cellar. He would kill two birds with one stone. One of them literally. He'd prepared the ground carefully. As it was turning out to be a beautiful spring, Richard had invited Alina for lunch and a drive in the afternoon, after they'd called in at the Barn and he'd gone over the books. "As long as we don't have to eat there," she had replied.

Richard had laughed. It certainly wasn't part of his plan that she should lunch there. "No, we'll drive along to Rye, just as the fancy takes us. We'll have a day off; Nicky will be fine at playgroup. We'll have a day to ourselves. Just the two of us."

Everything went beautifully according to plan. Richard was careful to discreetly set off from home with Alina at a time calculated to get them to the restaurant during the dead period of the morning. He was equally careful to check their arrival had gone unnoticed, as he quietly turned the Jaguar into the rear of the car park, near the usual spot. As expected, the place was quiet as a morgue. If they had been seen, he would simply have abandoned the plan and awaited another opportunity. As he locked the car, he handed the door keys to Alina, so she could admit them. Both sets of fingerprints were all over the car anyway, but Alina's would predominate on the back door keys. Still wearing his driving gloves, Richard entered the apartment. Mac and Janice were in the bar. He said: "I'm just going to check the last delivery down in the cellar; why don't you come and give me a hand?"

Alina followed him and when they reached the cellar door, Richard tugged it open and stood aside for Alina to descend. When she set foot on the first step, he pushed her forward with both his hands. She landed with a thump and he could see her head bleeding profusely. No one saw him push her and no one heard the fall. He waited a few seconds to make sure, then let himself out, leaving the door keys in the apartment.

It was now essential that he not be seen in the vicinity of the Barn, so Richard walked smartly to the taxi rank by the Imperial Hotel, and hired a cab to take him to the crossroads near his housing estate. That would be safer than being driven all the way home.

Sitting in the back of the taxi, he reviewed the morning's work: it had gone very well. He had no doubt Alina was dead. He had not gone down to make sure because he didn't want to leave evidence to show he had been down in the cellar that morning. He hadn't watched all those documentaries for nothing. Mac's prints would be all over the trapdoor, and traces to show they had all been around the apartment at sometime were to be expected.

Now Richard had to complete the plan. When he got home, he called the Barn to tell Mac he was too busy to make his usual visit and so had asked Alina to call in and bring the ledgers home. He replaced the receiver before Mac could start an argument. When Mac went back to the apartment, he would notice the open cellar door, and when he saw the Jaguar parked up and found no evidence of Alina about the place, his immediate response would be to go into the cellar, where a surprise would be waiting for him.

Richard waited impatiently for the phone call he was sure would come. The door bell rang. Two men in overcoats introduced themselves and eased their way inside. Inspector Collins invited Richard to sit down in his own lounge. After breaking the news, he continued: "We had a call from a Mrs Winthrop. She was practically hysterical. She found your wife's body in the cellar."

Richard shook his head. "What happened?"

"We thought you might be able to enlighten us a little on that score, sir. This Mrs Winthrop, she's your insurance agent, I understand?"

Richard nodded. This was decidedly odd. What on earth had she been doing at the Barn? Inspector Collins consulted his notes: "While looking out of the window of her office, over the road, she saw your car, a blue Jaguar with your personalized plaste, turning into the car park, with yourself at the wheel, at 11.20." he paused. Richard remained silent. The inspector continued: "She says she remembers the car; it's so distinctive, and apparently it was delivered one day while she was here."

Richard nodded like a man in a dream: a nightmare. The "yes" was almost inaudible.

"Apparently, sir, the bank has bounced a couple of direct debit payments on the insurance policy on your wife's life, so to bring it back in force, Mrs Winthrop thought she'd just go and have a quiet word with you. She went into the bar and enquired for you, since the place looked empty. The manager, Mr Macintosh, told her that you often call in unannounced to check over the books. Is that so, sir?"

Richard swallowed hard. "Yes, I do… but…" He couldn't finish the sentence. He knew what was coming.

"So they go into the back," continued Inspector Collins, "They see the cellar door open, but don't find you. He calls out. There's no reply. So they go down to the cellar. And, well, sir, I suppose you know what they found?"

Richard tried to pull himself together. "It was an accident. I mean, it must have been. Mac's always leaving that door open. I nearly fell down there myself one day."

"In that case, sir, why did you call the Barn to say you wouldn't be in today, when you'd already called in and gone away again?"

There was, of course, no answer to that question. That stupid woman Winthrop. And that damned car.

BE ASSURED

"That's why it's called life assurance," explained Joe. "It's the only thing in life that you're assured of." Greg had heard it all before, but Linda, who was new in the office, hadn't and was impressed.

"Wasn't it Ben Franklin who said that the only things in this world that were certain were death and taxes?" she joked.

"You mean that guy who used to be the manager over at Reliability Mutual?" queried Joe.

Linda looked as though she was beginning to have grave reservations about some of her colleagues, Joe in particular.

"And no wonder," thought Greg, casting a critical eye over his companion. Joe was about sixty and possessed a huge Irish family of children, or so it was rumoured. That was supposed to explain how, after a lifetime as a brilliant insurance salesman, he was still mortgaged up to the hilt and otherwise generally broke. Everything about him was seedy: his cheap shiny suit, his cheap cigarettes perpetually dangling from his full lips, his broken down wreck of a car. Greg had no intention of winding up like that. No sir. Not him. He was thirty, bright, chipper and full of confidence. Moreover, he was single.

"Can I ask you something on these pension forms?" Linda asked Greg.

Joe interrupted: "You don't want to ask him anything: he doesn't know enough to share around. How much did you make last month?" Before Greg could tell him it was about twice as much as Joe himself had earned, Joe continued: "You'd sell a lot more if you didn't have a tie like a dead kipper and a haircut like a lavatory brush." Greg and Linda exchanged knowing glances and went into a huddle at her table.

Greg had only recently returned to England from four years spent in Djakarta as a representative of the Imperial Petroleum Company, and he was finding it hard going. He didn't have any contacts, no close friends in the old country any more. Derek, the office manager, was always on at him to sell more to his friends and relatives, but he baulked at that. His relatives were mainly elderly and couldn't afford any extra expenditure. They simply didn't have the money. After wasting away a bit of time chatting, Greg and Linda adjourned to the Three Feathers for a pub lunch. It was the nearest pub to the office, and was run by a gay couple who served good genuine pub food at affordable prices. The only criticism was that it invariably contained Joe. Greg always marvelled at the way Joe moved between office and bar at opening time: faster than the speed of light. He could have sworn Joe had still been in the office when he and Linda had left, but as they entered, he was at the bar, waiting on an empty pint pot. "On the scrounge again," remarked Greg quietly with a nod in Joe's direction.

Linda was equal to the task. "I'll get the first round in," she offered, knowing full well that Joe would never accept a pint from a woman.

"I'll get a couple of plough-person's," quipped Greg. The stratagem almost worked, but not quite. After about fifteen minutes, when Greg and Linda were seated over their Cheddar,

Joe decided to join them. Worse yet, he started to lecture them on the best way to make a living selling insurance. "Telephones, that's what you want. A good three hours on the phone every day; one session in the morning to catch the businesses, one in the evening for the private punters."

"And a hide like a rhinoceros," remarked Linda, directly at Joe.

"Well we mustn't keep you from all your clients," added Greg maliciously. Their glasses were all empty. They remained so. Neither Linda nor Greg moved to the bar. Joe remained rooted. They sat and looked at one another. As it drifted into Joe's consciousness that he wasn't going to get a drink out of them, salvation hoved into view in the shape of Derek. Once more Greg was amazed an old man could move so fast.

"Thank God's he's gone," said Linda. "I find him really offensive sometimes."

Bearing in mind Joe's remarks about women in business,

Greg could well believe it. "Reminds me of my old boss out in Djakarta," he offered. "He was a sour sod and thick with it."

"I've often wished I'd travelled a bit more," replied Linda, "You know, lived in places, not just gone for holidays. Still, I've been to Bali. A couple of years ago. I loved it, but I wouldn't have thought it was much of a place for unaccompanied women. Mind you, I was OK I was with a crowd."

"Yes, it's certainly an interesting country," agreed Greg. "You know what you were saying about death and taxes? Well out there it's not true, not if they can help it. The taxation is minimal anyway, that's why they've got such lousy roads and water supplies, but most people just don't pay. They hang it out for years. The government simply haven't got enough tax inspectors to go round. When I was out there, there was a story going round that an ex-army general, who owned one of the small islands, set his face against paying, and when they finally got round to sending an inspector out to his private residence, the guy just disappeared. Never seen again. So the taxation office sent another one. He was found floating face down in the harbour at Djakarta. The next one got the message; he resigned rather than go after the general for his back taxes."

"What a place!" exclaimed Linda, duly impressed by this traveller's tale. "I definitely don't think I'd like to live there. But what about the police? What did they do about the tax inspectors?"

"I never heard," replied Greg. "But some of these rich types who own the islands and plantations are laws unto themselves. One of my friends at Imperial Petroleum disappeared out there," he added importantly. "No idea to this day what happened to him. Jack Colclough his name was. Mind you, he was daft; got himself involved with the local lovelies. One in particular was rumoured to have a rich daddy who wasn't too keen on Europeans. So he might have had Jack killed, or he might have run off with the lovely."

"But didn't the company do anything? Or the British Embassy?" asked Linda.

"On what grounds? There was no evidence that anything had happened to him, and with his reputation, it was just as likely he'd gone off on his own."

"But what about his family back in the UK? Didn't they do anything when they lost contact with him?"

"Apparently, according to the company's records, he'd only got an old father living alone somewhere and they didn't have much contact, just an occasional note at Christmas, that kind of thing. The old boy never contacted the company as far as I know," said Greg.

"What an exciting life you've led," chaffed Linda. Greg shrugged proudly. There was really nothing he could say to that.

When they drifted back to the office, Joe had buttonholed Graham, another of the new reps. "And so this guy never saw the client standing up; he was always sitting in front of the TV with a rug over his legs. His wife said it was to keep him warm. Anyway, as he's an old guy, they send him for a medical and he passes. All OK. No trouble at all. Then, after a few months the old boy dies. Old age? Accident? Not on your life. He was a smoker, see? A life-long smoker; he had coronary disease in a big way. It affected his circulation, see? And he died. Then it all came out. They'd sent his brother for the medical. Thought we wouldn't spot it; but we did, no problem. No doubt about it, the punters are a devious bunch, why I could tell you…"

But he couldn't. Young Graham was off. He didn't want to hear any more stories like that. Nor did anyone else. Linda and Greg hustled to their tables and pretended to be engrossed. Greg had recently purchased some share-holders' lists from Companies House and was flicking through them on microfiche to pick out those shareholders who lived locally. He would then send them a nice letter about his company's investment schemes, knowing that at least they had some money and had been willing in the past to invest it. And there it was: Mr Martin Colclough, Springbank, Nevers Road, Eastbourne. Martin Colclough, father of Jack. What a small world. Greg noted his address and wrote him a letter of a more personalized nature than the company's usual script.

A week later, the reply came in the form of a telephone call made to the office number. Mr Colclough would be pleased to welcome Mr Horrocks to discuss his investments. On the morning before the appointment, Greg swotted up everything he knew about investment, which wasn't much if the truth were to be told. But it was almost certainly more than Mr Colclough would know. Unfortunately, Greg was alone in the office with Joe.

"You don't want to waste your time with all that rubbish." Joe gesticulated in the direction of the instruction manuals. "Just get in there and do some business. When in doubt, sell 'em a five year investment plan. I always do. Never come away empty handed."

Greg had had just about enough of Joe. "I thought the idea was that we were supposed to offer them advice, help them get the most out of their money."

"Bugger that," countered Joe. "They've all got more money than we have, especially up in Nevers Road." He looked over Greg's shoulder. "Tell you what, I'll come with you, make sure you get a sale. For fifty per cent of the commission."

"Bugger that," said Greg.

By the time he got to Nevers Road Greg was beginning to wish he'd accepted Joe's offer. He'd got lost in the widely spaced roads comprising the luxury housing estate wherein Nevers Road stood. He was late and panicking. He needed this one. There weren't many others in the offing. When he finally found Springbank, he could hardly believe his eyes. It was a glass house. Literally. There appeared to be hardly any supporting structure for the huge double-glazed windows which surrounded both stories of the house. Mr Colclough was standing in what was obviously his lounge, looking out for Greg, and when he saw the car draw up in the road, he nipped to the front door to let him in.

Mr Colclough was very courteous and welcoming to Greg, and offered him tea and biscuits as soon as he was seated. Greg guessed that, like many old people living along this part of the south coast, Mr Colclough was lonely. He'd outlived his wife and his own brothers; he didn't get on with his wife's brothers and sisters, and he'd only got Jack, wherever he was. He welcomed a bit of young company, especially from a friend of

Jack's, who could tell him about his boy. Greg offered a carefully edited account of their time together in Djakarta, leaving out the local lovelies and tactfully emphasizing how highly Jack was held in esteem by the company and how busy he had always been. Mr Colclough, who was a small, bald man, wearing a bright yellow golfing pullover, was forgiving. "Of course, it's hard for young men to make their way in the world today. Not like it was in my day. Your word was good enough then. Now it's all papers in triplicate and computers. So I don't worry too much about him. No news is good news, eh?" Greg assented and was rewarded with a piece of Marks and Spencer's sponge cake. "But there is one thing, you know, that does worry me. It's why I asked you to come today. You see Jack is all I've got, so naturally I want to do my best for him. I'm not getting any younger. The old ticker isn't what it was. No cause for alarm, just *Anno Domini*, you know. Well, what I really want, is to do the best for Jack when I'm gone."

"Lucky sod," thought Greg. "Why can't I have rich parents?" Ah well, it was the luck of the draw and he really was fond of his parents, even though they'd never be able to leave him a bean. He said: "Of course, that's only natural."

Mr Colclough continued: "But taxes, you know. Inheritance tax, they call it, don't they?" Greg nodded. "Well, I've worked hard all my life and I don't see why the government should tax me when I'm dead. It's so unfair. I've already paid tax on my earnings and savings, and even on my pension. So what I want you to do, being a friend of Jack's and all, is to help me do what I have to do to avoid that tax."

Greg reeled. This was much better than he'd ever hoped it could be. What a relief he hadn't brought the sleazy Joe with him. That would have wrecked everything. Now he was being given the opportunity to sink well into Mr Colclough's financial affairs and, more importantly, his trust. Greg had learnt fairly quickly when he'd started in the financial services business that old people didn't trust casually or easily, but when they did trust, they did so without reserve. Whatever happened now, Mr Colclough was as good as his client. He would do his very best for him. Carefully and meticulously, he examined and noted Mr

Colclough's financial arrangements: the value of his house, antique Alvis car and furniture, his building society and bank accounts, his shares and insurance policies; even his minuscule credit card bill was duly noted. Greg promised to return in one week's time with a plan of action for Mr Colclough's perusal. After yet more tea, he walked to his car. It was going to mean a lot of work, but it would be well worth it. He might even ask Joe for advice, just to torture him.

The following morning in the office, Greg was working on his plan for Mr Colclough, when Joe hovered over him. "Make a sale then?"

"No, but I'm going to; a big one. Actually, I'd like your advice on inheritance tax mitigation." He waved the paperwork in front of Joe, so that he could see how much was involved.

"Pie in the sky," muttered Joe, who wasn't interested in giving real advice. He swerved off to pick on Linda.

Greg dutifully turned up in Derek's office and asked his advice. "So, you see, being a personal friend of his son, I'd like to do the best I can for him. He's living in a good district, belongs to the golf club and all that. If I can get in with that type of people, I'll be well away." Greg thought Derek would be pleased. After all, the company training scheme had emphasized the two-visit approach: the first was to be exploratory, allowing time before the next visit for the discussion of the case with the manager, if necessary, and the preparation of written quotations. It never worked out like that.

"You didn't sell him anything then?" asked Derek belligerently.

"No. How could I? I didn't know what to sell him for the best."

"What about life assurance. You should have sold him something. He'll have changed his mind by the time you get back."

"But there are ways of doing it and other alternatives. I want you to help me decide which is best."

Derek clearly thought all this was a waste of time. "Phone the specialists at head office, it's their job to sort out that kind of thing. I can't be expected to know everything." The trouble was, thought Greg, that Derek, like most of the other team managers in that office, didn't really know much at all. They had been over-promoted to managers on their abilities to shift expensive policies. They seldom knew much about what they sold. Joe leered at Greg as he came out of Derek's office and moved over to lecture Graham. Greg got on the phone to head office.

One week later, he was back in Mr Colclough's comfortable living room, explaining his carefully thought out plans. He gave Mr Colclough a couple of alternative schemes and talked them over with him. He didn't hurry the old man; he didn't press him. Mr Colclough was nobody's fool; he asked some very pertinent questions and mulled over the documentation, while they both drank Earl Grey and munched Walnut Slice. At length he said: "May I ask you a personal question?"

"Why yes," stammered Greg, carefully replacing the cup of perfumed tea.

"Are your own parents still alive?"

"Yes."

"Which of these plans would you recommend to them?"

Greg smiled. "I wish they needed to have either of them, but the problem simply doesn't arise. They've only got the state pension and they live over at Hove in a council flat." Then he added quickly, "But if they were in your position, I would recommend the second one."

"No doubt you have worked out the commission you will get for both of these plans?" twitted Mr Colclough.

"There's not really much difference," offered Greg. He reached for his briefcase. "I've got the calculations here somewhere."

Mr Colclough stopped him by putting his hand on Greg's arm. "It's all right, I don't really want to know. I don't expect you to work for nothing. If it does the job for me, that's all I want. You don't get anything for nothing in this world. I've lived long enough to know that."

Greg could feel a sale coming on. Whoopie! But he was to be disappointed. "Leave it with me, leave all the papers, and I'll think it all over carefully and let you know."

"OK. Fine," replied Greg, trying to hide his disappointment.

"I'll give you a call when I'm ready," said Mr Colclough.

"In other words, don't call me, I'll call you," thought Greg. They shook hands and Greg departed.

Sitting in his car in a lay-by on the main Eastbourne road, Greg felt sick. He'd blown it and he knew it. He'd had Mr Colclough in the palm of his hand and he'd let him go. He just couldn't be so aggressive as to press the old boy to sign. He knew well enough what would happen now. Mr Colclough would go down the golf club and chat it all over with his cronies. They would all know better than a trained financial adviser how to avoid inheritance tax: bank accounts in the Isle of Man, shares in the Cayman Islands. All useless ideas. All stupid. In the end, the best he could hope for would be that Mr Colclough would fall into the greedy hands of Barwell's Bank. The manager there would stitch him up good and proper, but at least his money would be relatively safe.

Greg crept into the office the next day, hoping not to be seen.

"Well?" demanded Derek.

"He's thinking it over, I'm…" But Greg got no further. Derek had very pointedly turned his back on him and stormed away.

"Told you," said Joe.

"Oh, I'm sorry," said Linda. Even Graham looked sympathetic. Greg buried himself in his shareholder's lists. Perhaps he wasn't cut out for this sort of thing. That lunch time, before going to the pub, he and Linda went shopping. He wanted her advice about a knitted hat and scarf he was thinking of buying for his mother. Linda was kindness itself and helped him choose a suitable style and colour. Not at all what he would have chosen himself, but doubtless better. He would cheer himself up with a surprise visit home that evening.

The following Monday, the third of the month, was a day of surprises all round. When Greg slipped into the office, Joe and Graham and some of the others were standing around in a small group, chatting. Greg found a memo in his pigeon-hole. They'd all got one. Derek had gone. He'd left the company.

Greg wandered over to the main group. "Well, he kept that quiet then. I wonder where he's gone?" he asked.

"Down the Labour Exchange," replied Joe.

"Why?"

"Office not doing the sales, that's why. The company give them a target and about a year to do it in. If they don't, they're out. I've seen it all before. Didn't I always say, what you need for sales is more telephoning? Stop wasting your time with those pansy shareholder's lists." Greg and Graham started to run.

At about eleven o'clock, there was a polite knock on the office door, and Mr Colclough appeared in the opening. Greg straightened his tie, parked his coffee mug on the floor under his table and went forward to greet the old man. Joe got there ahead of him. "Can I help you, sir?"

"I just want to hand in these forms." Joe almost grabbed them out of his hands. With any luck, the rep. wouldn't have signed his part of the forms and Joe could capitalize.

"To young Mr Horrocks," said Mr Colclough, smiling firmly. Greg stood politely to one side, waiting for Joe to disappear. Taking advantage of Derek's now empty office, Greg seated Mr Colclough and checked over the paperwork most carefully, especially the prepared trust forms. Everything was in order, and Mr Colclough had brought a building society draft for the correct amount. He really was a meticulous old gentleman. Greg had noticed that before: the elderly were precise in their habits and in their requirements.

"So, you're happy with them then, quite satisfied?" asked Greg.

"Oh absolutely, thank you," replied Mr Colclough. "I'm satisfied I've made the right decision. I went to my solicitor on Friday to make sure everything was in order with my will, so everything is all right now."

"Good," said Greg. "I'm pleased you're satisfied and I'll keep in touch with regular reports about that investment bond; you've made a wise choice there."

"I know," replied Mr Colclough easily. "I used to sell financial services myself you know, with the old Presbyterian

Life. I know when I've been given good advice, never fear." Greg laughed and the couple walked amicably towards the exit. Greg rather liked Mr Colclough.

He slipped back into the office to hand the paperwork to the manager. But there was the problem: there wasn't a manager to hand it to. "Poor Derek," thought Greg. "If only he knew." He was just wondering what he should do, when John Smart strode into the office.

"Oh God," said Joe faintly.

"Gather round," ordered the newcomer. They did as he bid. "My name is Smart, John Smart; some of you may know me." Judging by the pale looks on a few of the faces, some of them did. "I'm the new manager here. I'll be seeing you all individually in the course of the next two or three days, but this morning, I'll sign off any business that has come in and get myself settled in." It didn't take Mr Smart long to settle in; he seemed to have remarkably few personal office items but, being a Monday, there was a lot of business to check over and Greg had to wait quite some time before he got to see the new manager. In the meantime, he tried to pump some of the older reps. who clearly knew him. Even Joe seemed curiously reluctant to talk abut the new man, as if he could be overheard.

Greg's feeling of euphoria at his big catch faded within the first five minutes in Smart's presence. "Good," he said. "About time too." He flicked through the business register left over from Derek's time. "There's not been much else, has there?"

"Well no," agreed Greg cautiously. "I haven't been here that long, and it's taking a bit of time to establish myself. But I'm sure Mr Colclough will open a few doors."

"Well, let me tell you plainly, if you don't come up with a damn sight more than this in the next two or three months, you're out. I don't want time wasters." Greg was about to point out that he'd been working jolly hard, but Mr Smart rushed on; handing Greg a sheet of paper, which turned out to be an activity log for the week. He said: "Photocopy this for the next twelve weeks and follow the activities I've written out there, and we'll review your progress next month."

Greg was shattered. He'd never expected this. Unless you

had good personal or business contacts from the past, it was damned hard work building up a clientele. Smart must know that as well as anyone. But he just didn't care. He couldn't care less about helping his team members build their businesses; he wasn't prepared to encourage and wait. Judging by what had happened to Derek, he probably couldn't afford to.

Greg and the other reps. stood around disconsolately in the office. Most of the newer ones coming out of their interviews were holding the activity sheets. Some of the older ones were just having a good chewing out. The first real row came in the afternoon, after they had all been to the Three Feathers. Graham had even bought Joe a drink, as had many of the others, in the hope it would loosen his tongue. It did, but not, unfortunately, until his interview with John. No one heard what Smart said, but Joe stormed out, clutching an activity sheet. "I've been in this business longer than you have, matey, and if you think you can treat me like a trainee, you can bloody-well think again."

The first reasoned opposition to the activity sheets came from Linda. Apart from compulsory telephone sessions twice a day, and exhibitions and shopping centre visits at weekends, there were early morning and evening sessions devoted to door-knocking. Just going into a housing estate and knocking on doors to drum up insurance business. As Linda pointed out, this was dangerous for a woman: knocking alone on unknown doors was asking for trouble. John Smart didn't care: "If you can't do the job, get out." Some of the senior males in the office, together with Greg and Graham, supported Linda and tried to reason with him. It would, after all, reflect very badly on John himself, if anything happened to Linda as a result of following his instructions. He relented a little: "She can bring in the business some other way if she can, but she's got to do more."

Thus it was that the office settled down for two months of autumnal misery. Door knocking was a lousy job at that time of year, but even Joe participated. He couldn't afford to do otherwise. Graham left and went to agricultural college. Linda was next to go; she simply couldn't satisfy the rapacious demands for business imposed by the new regime. A couple of the old-timers left rather than be treated like office boys. Greg staggered on, with an increasing overdraft and the sword of Damocles over his head. He saw quite a bit of Linda; she was temping in a nearby office, and they started avoiding the Three Feathers. John now drank there at lunch times: he could afford to. Joe also did, but couldn't. Greg kept faith with his few clients, including Mr Colclough, dropping in from time to time with news of his investments, or simply for a chat.

Over lunch at the Crown and Anchor in November, Linda spotted an advertisement in the local paper: "Financial Advisers. Tired of The Hard-Sell? Call us for a company with integrity."

"What do you think?" she asked.

"No harm in giving it a try," replied Greg. "I may be looking for somewhere else myself soon; I'm never going to win with Smart in charge."

That afternoon, when her office was empty, Linda called the number, which turned out to belong to Novo Assurance, a relatively new company in the field, whose local manager expressed himself entirely in sympathy with the view that the financial services sector should help clients handle their money, not hard-sell and pester them. "A service industry," he explained. "Integrity, that's our watchword," he emphasized. Linda was intrigued and arranged an interview for the following Tuesday morning.

When she arrived at the small office over a bookshop, she was indeed pleasantly surprised as the manager explained the company's soft-sell ideas; and his ideas concerning the acquisition of clients were very much in line with her own. He explained how carefully he vetted his would-be reps. "To avoid the sharks, you know; we don't want them. I'll show you round." The grand tour lasted about five minutes, while the manager gently tried to pump Linda about her existing client bank, and until she spotted Derek on the telephone in the main office. She turned to the manager and said: "I see you've got Jaws working as a rep. I thought you didn't want sharks."

That evening, as she was relating the experience to Greg in

the Spring Garden Chinese Restaurant, he remarked, "It strikes me they're all the same." Linda agreed.

A few days later, Greg received a letter from Pont and Worthy, Mr Colclough's solicitors, asking him to contact them at their offices as a matter of urgency. All letters to reps. were opened and inspected by John Smart, and he called Greg into his office. "You'd better get on to this now; if you've made any cock-ups, you're for the high jump, sonny."

Greg was fairly confident that he'd done everything correctly for Mr Colclough, but, nonetheless, he was still anxious. When he spoke to Mr Pont himself, he was instantly reassured. Sadly, Mr Colclough had died, and the funeral was to be held in two days' time; would Mr Horrocks attend? There would be a short meeting after the funeral, in the offices of Pont and Worthy, at which the will would be read. Mr Pont hoped Mr Horrocks could be present. Greg expressed his condolences and said that, naturally, he would attend both the funeral and the meeting. He was genuinely sorry Mr Colclough had died. He'd come to like him.

Accordingly, Greg turned up for Mr Colclough's funeral in what he hoped was an appropriate suit and a dark grey coat, borrowed from his father. The weather had suddenly turned cold and the wind drifted in swirls through the cypress trees surrounding the large municipal cemetery. Greg met Mr Pont, who greeted him with interested courtesy, and noted that Mr Colclough was mourned by his neighbours and the members of his golf club, but not, apparently, by his son. Of Jack there was no sign. Greg was a little surprised and, as they walked back to Mr Pont's office, mentioned the fact.

Mr Pont coughed tactfully. "Mr Jack Colclough is… er… detained in Djakarta."

It was the way he said "detained" that made Greg think. That was why Jack had disappeared so completely from ken. He was in jail. Greg said: "I was out there a year or two ago, you know. We were both working for Imperial Petroleum and then he just disappeared."

"Unfortunately he took a sizeable amount of the company's funds with him, I'm afraid. They only caught up with him a few months ago. Apparently he'd been hiding out on one of the islands."

Greg raised his eyebrows and whistled softly. He'd heard nothing about it at the time. The company must have kept it quiet. "Did his father know? All we knew in our office was that Jack had disappeared."

"When we went through Mr Colclough's personal papers there was a letter from the British Embassy in Djakarta, informing him of his son's arrest. Mr Colclough transferred a sizeable sum out there to be help with legal fees and other… expenses." Knowing the local fondness for a bribe, Greg could guess the nature of those expenses. Mr Pont added drily: "When we informed the Embassy of Mr Colclough's demise, they replied with the address of the local lock-up. He'll be out in eighteen months."

The will itself proved to be a simple document. Apart from a few small bequests to friends and a larger sum in trust for Jack, "So that the size of the bequest will enable him to realize his undoubted talents and energy," the bulk of Mr Colclough's estate was left to Mr Gregory Horrocks, "In recognition of his industry, integrity and kindness."

Two months later, when Greg and Linda were sitting in the living room of the glass house, sorting through the late Mr Colclough's books and discussing the future, Linda suggested they form their own company: "Integrity Assurance. In memory of Mr Colclough," laughed Greg happily.

There was a knock at the door. Greg went. "Good evening, sir, I represent the Halcyon Life Assurance Company, and I'm just making a few calls in your area…" Joe, dripping wet, and for once not smoking, was half way through his spiel before he recognized Greg. "Thank you, but I don't think we need your services."

A LITANY OF LIES

The flight from New Zealand was long and tedious, and Lee's reading material was hardly designed to inspire confidence. "Verdict on Erebus", Justice Peter Mahon's account of the enquiry into the crash of an Air New Zealand plane in Antarctica, was an excellent book, but hardly, in the circumstances, reassuring. Lee put her book away and watched the clouds go by, glittering in the perpetual sunlight and casting their soft, coloured shadows only on one another and on the aircraft wings.

This was Lee's first journey to Europe and she was looking forward to it very much. She had been much impressed by Dr Rozetski's lecture at her university department in Christchurch, and he had apparently been much impressed by her. The two papers she had so far produced from her doctoral thesis had been well received; she was personable, and had asked Dr Rozetski a couple of intelligent questions at the end of his lecture. Her subsequent enquiries as to possible research positions in his lab. had been more hopeful than anything, but she had been pleasantly surprised by his enthusiastic response.

So here she was, flying down into Heathrow, ready to begin her three-year contract in a prestigious British university. When she finally staggered into the arrivals hall, she was dog-tired and unbelievably cramped. In vain she searched the crowded barrier for a familiar face. It wasn't there. Lee began to panic. Dr Rozetski had written to inform her that he had arranged accommodation for her, but had not specified where. Now, when she was at her lowest ebb, burdened with baggage well in excess of the allowance, and in a strange country, she was stuck not knowing where she should be going. After hanging about for a few minutes in the hope that Dr Rozetski would arrive, Lee visited one of the airport banks, obtained some small change from her supply of English money and tried in vain to find a vacant public telephone.

Just as she managed to edge her way into a cell, Lee heard her name echoing over the public address system. "Would Dr Lee Edwards from Christchurch please find her party at the meeting point."

She would be only too glad to. With great relief she pushed her trolley towards the signposted point. There she came upon Alan, a not particularly well-shaved, slightly balding man in his mid-thirties, who didn't look any too pleased to see her. "Dr Edwards? I'm Alan Hooper. The car's in the multi-storey."

As Lee struggled to heave her trolley-load towards the car park, Alan revealed that Dr Rozetski was in Manchester for the day, so he had been deputed to meet her. In a very few words he managed to create the impression that he regarded such a menial duty as a chore well beneath the status of a doctor of philosophy.

Once installed in Alan's battered Ford, Lee attempted to quiz him about his position in Dr Rozetski's team and the nature of the project upon which he was employed. She was unlucky. Alan, it appeared, was not a happy man. Driving past the university, he ungraciously offered: "I'll drop you off at your flat. You can get settled in and make your own way to the university from there tomorrow."

After a few mis-turns, Alan managed to locate the flat, situated in a small block containing, Lee would have estimated, about ten apartments in total. Surrounded by green, well-tended grounds and situated on a wide boulevard near a small shopping precinct, the block appeared to be quite pleasant. Finally Alan managed to get the keys to turn and admit them to the flat. Inside, it was very disappointing; there were a few tatty bits of furniture, including a sofa and a bed, but there was no cooker, washing machine or telephone.

Being situated on the second floor was a distinct disadvantage when it came to carting up the baggage, and Alan showed himself to be a true man by carrying up Lee's shoulder bag, leaving her to haul up the heavy bags. He dropped the keys on the scratched table and kicked the rucked carpet before saying: "Right then, I'll leave you to it. Dr Rozetski isn't expecting you until tomorrow."

"Thanks. Er… What's the best way in to the uni. From here?

"Dunno. You'll have to buy a car."

"I won't be able to get one in less than half a day, and besides, I don't really know where the university is in relation to where we are now. It's my first time in England."

Alan rubbed his upper lip. "We passed it on the way here. You'll have to get a bus or something. I don't know. You'll have to look out for a stop. I've got to go; I'm late for a doctor's appointment."

The following morning Lee set out at about a quarter past eight. When she located a bus stop there was already a long queue, and she surveyed her neighbours. Not having been in England before, she had not known quite what to expect, but she was disappointed in them. Many were badly dressed and not a few looked pinched and careworn. There was also a disproportionate number of children, clutching universally recognizable meal boxes in gaily coloured plastics. Their mothers were obviously dropping them off early at school before themselves going to work. As she rode away from her housing estate and towards the university suburbs the quality of the houses on either side of the route improved, as did the clothing of those getting on the bus.

After much wandering about the campus, Lee finally found the Biology Department, and was conducted by a flabby, pasty-faced porter to Dr Rozetski's lab. He was in his office and greeted her briefly and with the minimum of courtesy: "Good flight?"

"Not at all bad, thank you."

"I'll get you along to the main lab. And introduce you to Jackie, who's our technician. You'll be working with Alan, and we can get together about eleven to decide what you're going to do. Jackie can get you fixed up with building keys and equipment and all that."

Lee noticed that Dr Rozetski didn't enquire about her flat.

Jackie turned out to be a lad of about twenty-five, who looked more like a down-at-heel insurance agent than a qualified technician. However, he was friendly enough and, while showing Lee round the department and introducing her to the stores' personnel, showed his interest in all things Antipodean.

Lee asked: "Have you been working for Dr Rozetski long?"

"About six months."

"What did you do before?"

"Oh, this and that. I just fancied a change and the job came up, so here I am."

"You were lucky to have just the right qualifications."

"Qualifications? Oh yeh. I do day release up at the tech."

Lee didn't like the sound of this at all. She began to get the unpleasant feeling that life with the dour Alan and the unqualified Jackie might not turn out to be a bed of roses.

At eleven Lee, grasping the obligatory mug of coffee, joined Alan and Dr Rozetski in the latter's office. Alan still hadn't managed to shave; in fact he looked as though he hadn't even slept.

"So, Alan, how far have you got with that ATPase? Have you got the co-factors figured out yet?" Alan launched into a long convoluted explanation, the burden of which was that he hadn't finished even the preliminary part of the project. Dr Rozetski, who insisted on being called Jule, knitted his eyebrows together in displeasure. "I thought you were going to get at least somewhere with it yesterday."

"I never got round to it. After I'd finished at the doctor's, I had to pick Sylvia up from her job in the florists and take the kids to the dentist."

Jule lost his temper: "Alan, you'd better start getting some work done around here, or I'm not going to apply for any more money to keep you on."

Alan looked as though he couldn't have cared less. "Don't worry, Jule, I'll get it sorted out in a week or two. It won't hold us up. There's nothing much we can do until Lee gets going anyway."

For no good reason, Lee felt guilty, as though she was not pulling her weight, even though she'd only just walked in the door.

Jule outlined what he wanted her to do: basically she was to prop up the failing Alan: "working together", as he put it. This was not at all what Lee had anticipated she would be doing. It was nothing like the structural work in which her expertise lay and even less like the project outlined to her in Christchurch. She mentioned her reservations. Jule responded heatedly: "We can't get anywhere until we get this sorted out, and we're going to do that right now. I've got to give the powers that be something soon, so you'll just have to get on with it."

It wasn't until both Lee and Alan had departed Jule's office that she realized no mention had been made of what Jackie or, indeed, Jule himself, would be doing to further the great push.

In the weeks which followed, Lee found little time to consider what her fellows were up to. Jackie was around and about, popping up here or there, like a Jack-in-the-Box armed with a mobile phone. Jule was mysteriously busy for most of the time; Lee often saw him carrying test tubes and moseying in and out of the animal house. Occasionally losing his temper, he was obviously preoccupied with something, although Lee couldn't figure out what it might be. Alan continued to visit his doctor, dentist, wife's place of employment, children's school, or any other place which was not situated on the university campus. When he did turn up, he confined his activities to nit-picking and carping about Lee's work and capabilities.

Matters came to a head when Alan declared his intentions of buying a house. Now he added to his daily rounds a tour of the estate agents. Lee had reached the end of her tether; not only was she doing most of the work on this particular project, but she wasn't enjoying it. She was doing basic-grade technical work and she wasn't learning anything.

One day, however, she did learn something which interested her very much. Alan arrived at noon and announced that he and Sylvia had found a house. Jackie reached for his mobile phone: "You'll be wanting an endowment policy then, Al. I've got a friend who's a broker; he'll do you a good deal. I'll give him a call, shall I?"

Alan was disdainful: "No thank you, Jackie. If I wanted an endowment policy the last person I would buy it from would be a friend of yours. How is that blender working, Lee?"

"I'm surprised you care."

Alan sorted through a sheaf of paper-work and found a lilac coloured building society application form. "Got it. Anyone seen Jule?" Lee shook her head.

"What are you going to do with that, Al?"

"I've got to get Jule to sign it to confirm that I'll be working here for the next five years. It's on account of my being a contract worker."

"And you're going to ask Jule? Al, not even you can be that dumb."

Conscious of the fact that everyone in the department regarded him as inadequate, Alan was disproportionately offended by Jackie's remark. "I might remind you, Jackie, that I'm not dumb. Unlike you, I happen to have gained not only a degree, but a doctorate as well."

"True, and, also unlike me, you happen to have gone bust after you lost that last job at Saturn's. And, as for being dumb, well we'll just see whether the building society lends you the money, shall we? For a start, I don't see Jule committing himself to keeping you on here any longer than he has to."

Alan wasn't listening. He'd stomped off in search of the boss. Lee was interested. "What did you mean about Alan going bust after he lost his job?"

"Oh, I thought you knew, but I suppose, coming from New Zealand, you must have missed it. It caused quite a stir in some circles. Our Alan used to be in charge of a small department in Barking, that was until Saturn Pharmaceuticals caught him with his hand in the till. He'd been daft enough to abstract funds from the central office without bothering to purchase the equipment, so they fired him. It was all part of his get rich quick, internationally famous research scientist lifestyle. Al's problem was that he didn't have either the talent or the money to support the fantasy."

"Quite a history. I'm surprised Jule took him on after all that."

"Well, that's another story. It'll be quite interesting to see what happens when Al asks Jule for his signature on that form."

What did happen was a gigantic shouting match, which could be heard all over the third floor. Alan's voice featured prominently as he called Jule a bastard and a con-man. Following the slamming of a door, Lee heard Jule shout: "That's it, Alan. You're out."

Alan was seen to march along the corridor. "I'm going to see the dean. That'll get you fixed. Bastard."

"What an idiot."

Lee placed her rack of tubes on the bench. "Why is Alan off to see the dean? He surely can't expect any support from that quarter, given his work record here."

"That's yet another story. After Saturn Pharmaceuticals fired Al, he made a bee-line for Jule." Jackie hitched a stool under himself and looked innocent.

"All right, I'll fall for it. Why did Alan come to work for Jule?"

"Because Jule does research for Mother Nature Pharmacy, Saturn's big competitor. Now Al might not be too bright, but he had picked up a few useful ideas during his time with Saturn, and he'd learned all about Jule's little sideline. So he walked out of Saturn's orbit and into Jule's, God help him."

"I still don't understand why Alan thinks running off to the dean is going to do him any good."

Before Lee received an answer, Jule burst into the lab. "Alan Hooper no longer works here. Jackie, clear out his bench and cupboards and bring his personal possessions down to reception. He can pick them up on his way out"

"What about the grievance procedure? I don't think you can sack him on the spot like that, Jule, not without giving him a written warning first."

"Just do it."

"Right, boss."

Jule walked towards the swing doors; just before he reached them, he turned and addressed Lee: "If the dean asks, you just tell him how often that lazy shit took time off."

Lee didn't like the idea of becoming involved in Jule's quarrel with Alan. She said to Jackie: "I don't understand why Jule didn't get rid of him months ago."

Jackie, who was piling Alan's pens and old training shoes into a cardboard box, replied: "And the dean told him to get lost. End of stories."

Lee reflected that she wasn't even sure which one of the faces she saw in the tea room every morning belonged to the dean. He was clearly the kind of administrator who believed in the low key approach. Professor Kensington was, in fact, generally regarded by all who knew him as being selfish and preoccupied with his own research to an extent which precluded all other activities, including running the department.

To quell the row emanating from his secretary's office, the dean finally admitted Alan. Having lost the prospect of owning his own home and his job in the space of less than an hour, Alan was in no mood to bandy words. He gave Professor Kensington the benefit of his views on Dr Rozetski, his research and personality.

The dean was unimpressed, uninterested and frankly irritated. "If you insist, I can institute a grievance procedure, but it would be a formality. You wouldn't gain anything by it."

"Oh I see. All cut and dried, is it? Well, if you want to see your department smeared all over the national press, so be it."

At this point, Alan had anticipated that the dean would take the bait and ask what he meant. He didn't, for the simple reason that he already knew. "I doubt very much whether the press would be interested in the tittle-tattle of a research worker dismissed for unsatisfactory performance of his duties, especially one with your unfortunate history."

That morning Jackie and Lee did very little work. The episode with Alan had disturbed them, and Lee, in particular, alone in a foreign country, felt vulnerable. She had no one to turn to and was very grateful when Jackie asked her to join him for a beer and a round of sandwiches in the Gown and Garter.

It turned out that Jackie really understood how to treat a lady. As well as her cheese sandwiches, Lee was treated to a Scotch egg and a packet of crisps. After chatting on his mobile for a few minutes, Jackie opened the batting: "May, Prof Kensington's secretary, told me he gave Al the shove. Al threatened to call the press."

"Seriously, Jackie, I don't like all this. I'm worried. I didn't know Jule had any links with the cosmetics industry, or I wouldn't have come to work for him."

"Conscientious objector, eh?"

"I just think the whole industry is a waste of time. It uses up valuable research resources and it produces nothing of value. We've got all the cosmetics and grooming products we need; we don't need new ones. It's just profit-mongering. It's all so pointless."

"And cruel."

"It can certainly be if you use animals, which I presume Jule does; he's not a microbiologist. It's not the sort of project I want to be associated with, if only peripherally. Do you think the dean will have a quiet word with Jule and ask him to sever his links with Mother Nature Pharmacy?"

"Not he. Before they started funding Jule, they made good and sure they wouldn't get any flack from the university authorities. They came the old pals act and crossed the prof's palm with silver, so Al was on a loser from the start."

"It's difficult to know what to do for the best. If I nail my colours to the mast and quit, I'll have to go back to New Zealand, and there aren't any openings for my kind of research out there. Ideally, I'd like to get another contract over here, but I have a feeling that if I walk out on Jule, he would be nasty enough to give me a stinking reference. He strikes me as that kind of guy."

"Another one?"

"Not for me thanks, Jackie." Jackie drained his pint and brought her back a half just the same. "How did you find out about Jule's connection with Mother Nature?"

"I just kept my eyes open. He was always scuttling in and out of the animal house and doing bits of experiments on his own, so I had a few words with Alf, the chief technician over in the animal house. Jule had given him instructions that certain of his animals were to be kept apart from the others and given different regimes. Alf said that sometimes he gets calves arriving in crates stamped on the outside with Mother Nature's head office address. Usually, when that happens, he gets a consignment of chemicals through the stores a few days later, and then he takes off doing his own thing for a few weeks." Jackie pointed a knife at the Scotch egg: "Don't you want that?"

"Just half would be fine." Lee bisected the egg.

Jackie wolfed down his half. "When we get back, I'll take you down and show you."

"I'm surprised the animal house technicians don't kick up a fuss."

"What can they do? They have a grouse now and again, but they're all afraid for their jobs. The dean has made it plain where his sympathies lie, and you've seen what Jule is like when he losses his temper."

"But why does Jule do it?"

"For the money. Why else? It's part of the brave new world. Learning and knowledge for their own sakes are out. The commercial world is in. More and more departments are becoming entirely dependent on business for their research funding. In effect, they're just a cheap way for interested companies to get their research done. They've sold their souls. The new breed of researchers these days don't look upon it as a vocation, they just look upon it as a means of getting rich. The integrity has gone out of it."

Lee was inclined to agree with Jackie's analysis, it had been just the same in New Zealand, but she was surprised to hear him making it. She resolved to spend the afternoon looking through the job vacancies in the journals.

Jackie polished off the crisps. "Well, us poor folk had better get back to earning our crusts before Jule decides to fire us all. We can walk through the animal house on the way back."

As they walked down the corridor towards the rooms holding the larger animals, Lee petted the rats. In a rear compartment Jackie pointed to a couple of calves huddled in a crate and to a small selection of rabbits. "He doesn't look to have too much on the go at the moment. He usually has more rabbits." Jackie affectionately patted the calves. Lee felt sorry for them. Using animals for medical research for the benefit of mankind was one thing in her view, using them for trivialities was quite another.

"I'm surprised at the dean giving his permission for this kind of effort. OK, even if he did get a sweetener from Mother Nature Pharmacy, it's a very dangerous thing to do, I would have thought, especially in the current climate of animal liberation movements and all that. After all, the buck stops with him. He's the head of department. If this were all to come to light, the department, and he, in particular, could be in for some very bad publicity."

"Only if it could be proved that he knew. He could always deny it."

"I suppose so, but Mother Nature Pharmacy wouldn't be shelling out to keep Jule going without a written assurance from his head of department that the necessary facilities would be made available to them, you know, the basic kinds of things: glassware, bench-space, support services, centrifuges."

"Jule bought that centrifuge from their money. But I take your point. You reckon that Prof. Kensington must have given them written permission somewhere along the line?"

"Certainly."

"Interesting."

As Jackie and Lee reached the rear entrance of the Biology Department they espied Alan, leading a bearded young man bedecked with cameras and carrying what looked like a portable tape recorder. Jackie nudged Lee: "Oh aye. Keep your head down and don't talk to any strangers this afternoon. That's Richard Elton from the local rag. Old Al's about to kiss and tell."

Lee was horrified. The last thing she wanted was to be featured in the press as being associated with a somewhat disreputable enterprise she didn't even approve of. Fortunately, it never came to that. Alf spotted Richard Elton attempting to take a flash photograph just inside the animal house. He got a couple of his larger colleagues and ejected Alan and the journalist before too much material had been gathered. He also informed the dean, who instructed his secretary to inform security and Dr Rozetski, in that order.

Lee was staring out of the lab. Window when Richard Elton was led away. "Will they call the police?"

"I doubt it. The last thing they want is to get the cops on campus. Apart from it creating a bad image of the university, there are laws concerning the housing and treatment of animals, and I bet Jule is breaking a few of them. They wouldn't want any independent witnesses. You got a camera?" he asked, with seeming irrelevance.

"No, I'm afraid not. I mean I have, but not here. Why?"

Jackie wandered out of the lab., presumably in search of a camera.

The following morning Lee bought a copy of the *Examiner*. Front page prominence was given to a photograph of two sad-eyed, cute calves. All things considered, the accompanying text was restrained and well-balanced. An attempt was made to point out that it was consumer demand which drove the search for "newer" and "better" cosmetics and household products. Readers were reminded that the university was a major local employer and that non-animal testing was not without its limitations and dangers. Lee wondered about the identity of the quoted "scientific expert". She noticed that several of her fellow passengers on the bus were skipping the text and commenting unfavourably on the photograph.

Wending her way up the paved path towards the main entrance of the Biology Department, Lee espied the unprepossessing sight of Professor Kensington reading a statement to a group of bored-looking journalists. Jule was nowhere in sight. Lee's path was effectively blocked by the crowd, so she hung about, well away from the assembled cameras.

The dean was droning on: "So I can categorically state that no member of this department has any contract with the Mother Nature Pharmacy Company. It is my opinion that Mr Elton no doubt acted in good faith upon the information he was given. This information unfortunately stems from an employee recently dismissed for absenteeism. The case is all the more sad since the employee in question, Dr Alan Hooper," the dean paused to make sure the journalists had all got the name, "has been previously dismissed for theft from the pharmaceutical company which then employed him, and was given the post here largely on compassionate grounds, to help him rebuild his career. That is all I have to say, gentlemen."

"What about Dr Rozetski?"

"Dr Rozetski is a scientist of international reputation, who continues to enjoy my complete confidence in his integrity and abilities." Professor Kensington made an undignified entrance into his department, leaving the journalists to besiege his gates. Lee slipped inside and up to the third floor.

She saw Jackie looking out of the window overlooking the animal house. A few of the journalists were attempting to gain admittance to the complex. "They ain't there."

Lee hitched herself into her lab. coat. "Eh?"

"Jule got rid of the calves and rabbits last night when everyone had gone home. God knows where he's got them now, but they're not in the animal house. It looks like they're going to make a mug out of Al."

Lee hadn't liked Alan; she had found him lazy and boorish, but he had spoken the truth about Jule and his sidelines. "Professor Kensington was giving a press call as I came in and he was doing his best to blacken Alan. I can't see him ever getting another job in science after that, poor devil. He wasn't particularly honest, and he wasn't even a good scientist, but he did have a point."

Jackie opened the window and shamelessly listened to the comments of the journalists, floating up from outside the animal house. Some of them were expressing their displeasure at not being allowed to interview Dr Rozetski. Jule stamped into the lab. and practically shut the window on Jackie's head.

He called Lee over and addressed them both. "I expect you've seen that crap in the *Examiner* this morning. Now I don't know where they got their information from, but I intend to find out. In the meantime, I want you two to keep your mouths shut. Don't go giving any interviews. Don't get mixed up with things that don't concern you. Understand?"

Lee was tired of Jule's unpleasantness. She asked: "What do you mean 'find out who is responsible'? You know who it was. Alan had that journalist up here yesterday."

"But Alf said he didn't get into the back of the animal

house. He couldn't have taken those photographs of the calves."

Jackie whistled. "Elementary, my dear Watson."

The devil took Lee. "As a point of interest, Jule, what were you doing with those calves? We don't use calves on this project, so why do you need them?"

"How I chose to conduct my own research programme is no concern of yours. I pay you to work on this project, not to question me."

"But you do have a contract with a cosmetics company, I presume?"

Professor Kensington made the situation clear in his statement to the press this morning and don't you attempt to suggest otherwise."

"But Jule…"

"But nothing. You get on with your own work, that's what you're paid for. How is that ATPase coming?"

"Not too bad, but that's not the point. If I had known about your links with Mother Nature, I wouldn't be working here at all. I feel like you've conned me. When we met in Christchurch, you told me I could do structural work if I came to your lab., not this basic-grade biochemistry. And besides, if I'm doing the work, I have a right to know what it's all in aid of. I don't necessarily want my efforts to go for the greater good of face creams." For Lee this had been a relatively long speech and she looked at Jule to see how it had been received.

His face was stony: "If you don't like it, you can get out. There are plenty of others who would be grateful for your job, and don't you forget it."

After Jule had left the lab. Lee asked Jackie: "What are you going to do? Will you stay on here?"

"Not me. I've done enough here, so I'll be off at the end of the month."

Missing the significance of Jackie's words, Lee asked: "Does Jule know?"

"No, I'll just quit and lose the salary. What about you?"

"I'll be off too as soon as I can get anything else. It's not just the kind of research he does, it's the way he treats me, like some disobedient five year-old."

"Good for you. Will you be going back to New Zealand?"

"Probably. I reckon it might be my best chance, even if I do have to change fields. I'll be on my home territory, and that's always a help, because I don't reckon I'll be getting any from Jule."

Jackie winked: "Well, you never know, I might be down there myself someday. I understand it's a very interesting country."

"Come and look me up."

"Love to. Thanks. I wonder if our little local difficulties have hit the radio." Jackie tuned his portable radio away from his favourite music station to the local news and phone-in channel.

"…And the Mother Nature chain has denied any link with the University of Broxton, but our reporter, Belinda MacIntosh, has discovered the existence of a contract between the dean of the Biology Department, Professor Kensington, Dr Rozetski and Mother Nature Pharmacy Company, whereby the dean agreed to the provision of certain departmental research facilities and Dr Rozetski undertook to carry out a research contract on the company's behalf."

"Oh ho. He fell right into that one, didn't he?"

"How do you mean?"

"The dean. He and Mother Nature Pharmacy must have thought they'd got away with it. Jule shifted the animals, and all they had to do was deny everything. They didn't think Alan had any proof, so they got their heads together and decided to conceal the truth. What might be referred to as orchestrating a litany of lies."

"An interesting choice of phrase, and not, I would have thought, a very well known one. How did you come across it? I didn't know Peter Mahon's book was available in this country."

"I studied the case when I was doing my law degree. I thought you might appreciate the phrase, being a Kiwi."

"You're a lawyer?"

"Of sorts. I prefer the term "Seeker of Natural Justice."

At this point, Jule crashed back into the lab. "I don't know which of you took it, but it doesn't matter. You're both fired. Get out."

Jackie replied: "I doubt whether, on the evidence you could bring, you could justify dismissing either of us, but I'll make it easy for you. I took that photograph of the calves and I photocopied the contract that you and the dean signed with Mother Nature Pharmacy."

"Those documents were confidential."

"Then you shouldn't have left them lying about in an open desk drawer; but it doesn't matter, I'll be on my way now."

Lee added: "And so will I, and in case you're going to threaten me with wrecking my career, please be my guest. In the circumstances, a bad reference from you would be the greatest boost you could give me."

Jackie picked up his mobile phone. "Two one-way flights to Christchurch for next Saturday? British Airways?"

Lee replied: "Fine by me."

A PORTRAIT OF ANNIE

Andy walked slowly back from Barnthorpe's towards Dodgson Street. He'd managed to get off a bit early today and the sun wasn't down yet. He'd get his mum to give him a quick sandwich tea and then he'd be off to The Edge; the sunset should be just right. As he walked along Crimea Terrace he could see Annie in the distance. She lived just around the corner from Andy and she was always there, just sitting on her washed front step. He gave her a wave. She nodded back and lit herself another cigarette.

Andy stood on the step of number four and inserted his key into the lock. The fragile front door pushed open easily and he was in his parents' tiny front parlour. "That you, love?" called his mother.

Andy resisted the temptation to ask "Who else?" and replied: "Yes. I got off a bit early. With any luck, I'll be able to get off to The Edge before the sun sets."

"Oh I don't know about that, love, I haven't got the chops on yet. Did you have a good day?" Muriel Duckett bustled into her immaculate lounge and picked up Andy's discarded anorak, brushing it down as she took it to the small cupboard by the coal hole.

"Look, Mum, I'll just get myself a sandwich and be off, otherwise I'll never get that canvas finished."

"Oh no, love, you've got to have your tea."

Andy's heart sank. He was heading for the usual destructive argument. "Look, mum, I'll be fine. I can have the chop later, when I get home. If I hang around now the light will be gone." He could hear the whine in his own voice.

"Now you know what I think about that, Andy. I always gave your father a good hot meal, when he was working. You've got to eat."

"I will be eating, Mum."

"No, love; I mean all of us sitting down together, having a proper meal."

It occurred to Andy that he was sure Picasso's mum had never insisted he ate pork chops.

Andy's father shambled into the parlour and plumped himself in front of the television. Reaching for the *TV Times*, he asked: "All right, Andy?"

"Fine, thanks, Dad. How have you been today?" He knew what the answer would be.

"Same as always, son." Every day was the same now. He wasn't an old man, but he looked like one. He no longer worked; he'd retired on ill-health grounds. Nowadays he just spent his time sitting in front of the television or pottering down to the Dog and Whistle.

Andy ran lightly upstairs and into his miniscule bedroom at the back of the house. He rummaged about under his bed for his painting gear, changed into a thick sweater and a pair of old, paint-stained trousers, and ran down to collect his anorak. As he paused by the entrance to the back kitchen, he could see his mother eyeing the grill on the gas stove. "Don't do one for me, Mum. I'll do mine when I get back. See you later."

Andy's father wheezed from the parlour: "You're not going out." It wasn't a question; as usual, it was an order.

Andy tried to avoid a shouting match: "I've got to get over to The Edge, Dad. I want to finish this canvas before the light goes."

"Your mother's doing chops and you're going to sit down and eat them. We always have a meal together at the end of the working day."

"It won't be more than half an hour, love."

"Look, Mum, it's just the once, and I've got to get this finished. OK?"

Ted shifted uncomfortably in his armchair. "Damn waste of time. I don't know what's the matter with you, Andy. When I was your age I was doing overtime and of a Friday night I was going to the flicks or the Mecca."

Andy knew it was a mistake, but he had to defend himself.

It was important to him that his parents understood his need to paint, that it was the most important thing in his life, much more important than Barnthorpe's or the pub. "Dad, painting is important to me. It's not just a hobby, it's what I want to do, more than anything else."

His father coughed for several minutes. The asbestosis had left him unable even to maintain a conversation, let alone do anything physically active.

"Are you all right, Dad?"

"Now don't you go upsetting your father, Andy. You know it goes straight to his chest." Muriel was carefully setting the table for three.

"I'm not upsetting him, Mum, or you, come to that. I'm just trying to point out that I'm twenty-three and I'd like to have a little life of my own."

Ted had recovered his composure enough to argue again: "When you start paying your way around here, then you can start having a life of your own, as you call it. Why don't you ask Barnthorpe's about getting a bit of overtime? I can't understand what you've got against the place. There's plenty round here would be glad of a job there. If you got overtime you could give your mother a bit more every week and still have some left over in your pocket of a Friday night."

"There's more to life than working in a cotton mill, Dad, or at least there is for me. Overtime doesn't exist these days, and I don't want to spend every evening in the pub, like you used to." Andy threw on his anorak and slammed out of the front door.

His father didn't seem to have noticed: "Barnthorpe's was good enough for your uncle Frank. Reilly's was good enough for me for thirty years. I don't see why working in a factory isn't good enough for you. You could earn good money if you put your mind to it."

"There, there; now Ted, don't get all upset. He'll be back when he's done his painting. I'll get him something then."

Muriel went over to her tiny front window and, with the front of her apron, absently polished the china dog reposing there. She saw her son wave to Annie again. She was still sitting on her step, watching the sun throw its colours over the sky.

"That Annie's still on her step, Ted. She's always there, poor girl. Oops. I can smell burning." Muriel hurried back to her kitchen.

"Annie isn't a girl, she's a grown woman. She's nigh on thirty. I don't know what's wrong with her. Why does she want to sit there all the time? Why does she want to live there all on her own anyway?"

Muriel served the chops and Ted managed to struggle over to the minute Formica dining table. "If he's not here, I'll eat his chop." Muriel loved Ted or, at least, she thought she still did, even after all the years of crippling ill-health and drinking, but she loved her Andy even more. She firmly removed the third chop and placed it in the refrigerator, out of harm's way.

Over the meal Ted reverted to a favourite theme: "Like all the young today, he is; they don't want to work. I was married when I was his age, and you can't tell me that Annie Duvitski's up to any good, living on her own like that. We all know why single women like that want their own places. Why doesn't she get married?"

"Oh Ted. Annie's ill. She's got that depression. You know she has. That's why the council gave her that place, on account of her not being able to fend for herself. That's why she gets the social, because she can't work."

"Can't work? Of course she can work; there's nothing wrong with her. It's all in her mind. It's because of folk like her that people like me, people who've worked all their lives, can't get enough to live on when they're ill. I worked thirty years for Reilly's, until they finished me with the bronchitis and I couldn't work no more. And she's never worked a day in her life, and she gets the same as me. It's not right."

These days Ted's appetite wasn't as good as it used to be, and Muriel was always careful to avoid rows at meal times, lest his ulcer be provoked. Eating her sprouts in dignified silence, she reflected that, in his younger days, Ted himself had been no angel. Of course, a lot of his troubles had been due to his job. Working with asbestos had been a well paid job, one Ted had first learned to do in the 1950s, but it was thirsty work, and Ted had spent a great deal of his wages and overtime pay in the

Dog and Whistle. Muriel had not had an easy life and she thought Andy had suffered too. When he had first gone to school, his parents had been able to pay for him to attend a private Catholic boys' school. Then, as Ted had grown older and less fit, his bonuses and overtime payments had dropped. Given a choice between Andy's education and showing an open hand down the pub, Andy had lost the contest, without too much of a struggle on Ted's part. By the time Andy had reached his teens, Ted had been showing the first signs of serious illness and was encouraged by his employers to take a job in the stores, where he would not be exposed to the raw asbestos itself. The drop in salary and status had been so demeaning that Ted had refused and continued to work in the milling room. Ted's finances had continued to decline with his health, and even Muriel had begun to notice the gap in living standards that had opened up between her family and the others she knew. She thought Andy had felt it too and had often wondered if he would have turned out differently if they'd been able to buy a house on one of the new estates and send him to college. Even today she worried that the reason Andy never brought his friends home was because he was ashamed of living in a council terrace that had been built in 1910. Muriel thought she could trace this change back to the time when Andy had gone to the secondary school, when their fortunes had significantly begun to fail. He had always been a happy little lad when he'd been at St. Patrick's, but when he'd gone to Royal Road Secondary he'd started to withdraw into himself and become artistic.

While Ted and Muriel were polishing off their gypsy tart and planning their evening's viewing together, Andy was settling himself on his regular patch of grass overlooking The Edge. The Edge was not a natural geographical feature, although no one seemed to understand what had caused its formation. It was, in fact, a sharp cliff, formed by the rapid subsidence of one half of Victoria Terrace. The remains of the terrace of houses could still be seen at the base of the escarpment. While this gave the current inhabitants of the houses on the remaining side of the street a wonderful view over the allotments and two disused mills, it did nothing to add to their sense of security. Rossdale Town Council had issued dark warnings about the effects of mining in Victorian times, although it was never stipulated exactly who had mined exactly what, in the middle of the town. The local historical society had found evidence of an underground stream and Reilly's Asbestos Works had firmly declared the subsidence to be nothing to do with them, not that anyone had thought it was.

Andy, now firmly seated on his camping stool on a patch of grass that had once been some poor soul's front garden, painted away. The sunset was marvellous; the colours were the best he had ever seen: a clear red and pink, which appeared to float in bands, like coloured islands in the sky. He was surprised how well it was going. Usually when he'd had an upset at home or work, he couldn't settle, but this evening was an exception. It was remarkably warm and pleasant on The Edge, and at least he was out of the house. Increasingly these days he enjoyed getting away from the company of his father.

By seven he had almost finished and sat back to admire his work, considering whether he should add the finishing touches now or on Saturday. He didn't want to make a mess of the painting now because he was too tired. His mind began to wander. The painting was going really well these days, a couple more and he would have enough for that exhibition Jacob Mercer had promised him. Mercer had been very keen on the canvases he'd seen in April and had promised him an exhibition in his Manchester gallery, provided he could produce enough material.

Andy decided to leave the finishing off until Saturday; instead he sat and looked out over the disused chimneys. Harrison's had finished first, and then Blinkhorn's had gone two years later. He wondered how long it would be before Barnthorpe's closed their doors for the last time. When they did, it wouldn't bother him, he'd be on his way by then. He'd be set up by Mercer's exhibition and, although he never expected to be wealthy, he could reasonably expect to pick up enough commissions to make ends meet, once he got well enough known. A cloud passed over his horizon. His father wasn't going to last long and he started to worry about his mum. How would she cope when he'd left home?

One of the locals from Victoria Terrace strolled up behind him: "Nice view that, lad. A good bit of work."

Andy turned round and saw a small, ruddy-faced man accompanied by a Yorkshire Terrier. "Oh. Thanks. Do you think so?"

The note of pride in Andy's voice appealed to the elderly gentleman. "Yeh, I reckon I do, lad. Do a lot of paintings, do you?"

"Yes; quite a few. I'd like to do some portraits, but it's a bit difficult to get people to sit for you, so I've done more landscapes, town views and all that."

"Well you keep at it. You've got a nice little touch there, lad. You'll never want for a living." The man lifted his trilby and strolled off into his precariously placed living room.

Andy gathered up his materials and set off for home. That elderly man had lifted his spirits in a way that his parents had never done, could never do. His mum tried hard, but she had never understood, and his dad simply didn't care. That much had become clear when the chance of a place at art school had loomed. Ted had put his foot down hard: "I'm not going to go on supporting you to go messing about drawing pictures. I left school when I was fourteen and it never did me any harm."

Andy thought that even to this day, even when he was dying of asbestosis, his father probably still believed that. To everyone else it was obvious that working at Reilly's had been his death sentence, just as working at Barnthorpe's had killed his brother. Frank had been tending the machines one day when part of the housing of one of them had broken lose and fallen onto him. His left leg and chest had been crushed; he hadn't stood a chance. And this, thought Andy, was his father's idea of a good employer.

As he rounded the corner, Andy saw Annie getting up off her step. The evening was quite cool now and she was going in for the day. He knew she would spend the rest of the evening watching television, just like his parents. He thought of the little he knew of Annie: she had lived in number three as long as he could remember. She was always on her own. She'd never worked, and had never had anyone living with her. Suddenly Andy knew where he could get a model for a portrait. Annie would be ideal. She had a quality of stillness and emptiness that appealed to him, qualities he would never be able to find in a professional model, qualities he thought he could show to the world in his painting. And it would be company for her; she might even enjoy sitting for her portrait. It would give her something to do. If she wanted, he would give her a second small portrait of herself by way of a "thank you". Andy thought that would mean more to her than money: it would show her that someone cared, that someone took an interest in her.

As he entered the front parlour, he braced himself for the continuation of the row. "You took your time; where have you been?"

"Up at The Edge, painting."

"In the dark? Anyway, what's to paint up there?"

Andy unwrapped his painting and held it up.

"It's very good, son, but wouldn't it be better if you did nice scenes, like the moors or Hollingbury Lake, or something lie that?"

"Mum, the point of it is that it's real life. A real old industrial scene, not a prettified tourist scene."

"Waste of time."

"Oh forget it, Dad." Andy went to his room, stowed his painting equipment and propped the painting against the side of his little wardrobe. He returned to the kitchen. "Where did you put my chop, Mum? I'll do it myself now."

His mother heaved herself from in front of a repeat of Steptoe and Son and followed him into the kitchen. "Don't you fret yourself, son, I'll do it, and I'll boil up the potatoes and sprouts again."

"Thanks, Mum. Are you sure?"

"Your mother's got better things to do than run round after you all the time. I want my Horlicks."

The following day was Friday, the last day of the working week at Barnthorpe's. Long gone were the days when there was

Saturday morning overtime for all who wanted it. Andy just made it to the time clock before eight. Another eight hours of mindless boredom beckoned. During the morning his idea for Annie's portrait developed in his mind. He resolved to ask her on his way home from work this evening. With any luck he could make a start in the morning. She wouldn't be going shopping; she rarely did. If the weather was fine, she would just be there, sitting on her step, smoking endless cigarettes. It would be a portrait of emptiness, loneliness, sadness. The wraith-like Annie Duvitski would sit on her step, looking out over the world for all eternity.

At lunch time Andy joined Mark and Paul down the pub. Mark wasn't any too happy about the way things were going at Barnthorpe's. "They're not keeping the stores full like they used to. You can always tell. It was the same when I was up at Mason's. I reckon another couple of years at the outside. Still, I'll be all right, I'm off at the end of next month to join my brother-in-law in his garage."

Paul didn't think he would be that lucky: "I was on the dole for six months after I left college, and I've still got a whacking great loan to pay off. If this place closes down, I'll be right in it. What about you, Andy?"

"I want to be a painter. I mean, I am a painter. Mercer's have offered me an exhibition if I can get another couple of good canvases together. When I've done that, I'll be off, so it won't worry me too much."

"Lucky sod. You'd never believe it, but I'm a fully qualified civil engineer and this was all I could get." Paul stared into his empty glass.

"Want another half in there?" asked Mark. "Still, Andy, if you hit on hard times, you could always do a bit of re-spraying for me and Mitch, at least you'd know more about paint than most people."

In the gloom of a wet afternoon, Andy's mind ranged around for another subject for a portrait. He looked around at his fellow workers. Was there a canvas there? No, he couldn't see it; it wasn't there. The title grabbed at him. "Watching the World Go By". Perhaps he could do a series. Yes, that was it. A series of people just watching their world's go by. Annie would be the first, then there could be tourists on the prom. at Blackpool; old people, looking out of their front windows; tramps on park benches. An endless stream of creativity flowed before him.

On his way home Andy walked over the road and had a quick word with Annie. He sat down beside her and accepted a cigarette. "How's things, then?" he asked.

"Just the same, you know." She didn't ask him how he was. She wasn't interested. She wasn't interested in anything.

He volunteered: "Things are a bit slow down at Barnthorpe's right now."

Annie exhaled. "Oh."

"You know I do quite a lot of painting and sketching, Annie? Well, I was wondering if I could paint a picture of you."

"What do you want to paint me for?" It was the first sign of animation Andy had ever seen her display.

"Well, I like painting people and things around me, real places and real people. It's like painting a history of Rossdale, our town and our way of life. Us as we are."

She looked at him with mild interest; he thought he'd struck a chord in her, possibly the first one that had ever been sounded. "Yeh, you can paint me if you like."

"Oh thanks, thanks a lot. It's really important to me. Great. Thanks." Andy coughed; he wasn't much of a smoker. "I couldn't offer to pay you anything for the modelling."

"That's all right. I haven't got anything else to do."

Andy knew that, but he continued: "But I could do a little painting of you, a second one, for you to keep. If I ever get to be a famous artist, it might be worth quite a bit, but anyway, you'd have an original portrait of yourself. Not many folk have got one of those, especially round here."

"Thanks." She'd lost interest again. Her eyes were wandering over the road to where a dog was nosing in the gutter.

"Could I come round tomorrow? Tomorrow morning?"

"Yeh. O.K. Then."

"About ten suit you?"

"OK." Annie flicked ash onto the pavement.

Andy stood up awkwardly and added: "You wouldn't have to do anything. I'd just like to paint you as you normally are, sitting on the step."

"Fine."

"Thanks then. I'll see you tomorrow."

Andy's euphoria lasted only until he entered the front parlour of number four. He saw the problem at once. His father was sitting looking out of the window. He had been looking across the crossroads and had seen his son talking to Annie. "What you talking to that Annie for? What did she want?"

"She didn't want anything, Dad. I want to paint her and I went over to ask if I could do a portrait of her, sitting on her step like she always does."

Muriel bustled through into the parlour. "Fish all right, son?"

"Great, Mum."

"Why do we always have to have fish on Fridays? We're not Catholics."

Muriel ignored her husband. She had started serving fish on Fridays when Andy had been at St. Patrick's and, tenacious of habit, had never ceased, even though most Catholics had. She had had a very trying day, although Andy was not to know this.

Seeing his father sitting at the window had given him the idea for the second painting in his series. He would do a portrait of his own father, sitting in his own parlour, with his oxygen cylinder parked by his chair, his face set with disagreeable resentment. There was no time like the present. Unwisely, Andy decided to try his luck: "Yes, it'll be part of a series, Dad. I want to do some portraits of local characters, portraits of real, working class people."

His mother interrupted: "That's a nice idea, Andy, isn't it, Ted? You don't get many ordinary folk in picture galleries, I mean you don't see them in the paintings."

Ted turned his mottled face towards his wife. "That's because they can't afford to have their pictures done, woman. The people what's in them paintings, they pay for 'em. Who's going to pay for a portrait of me or that Annie? She hasn't got any money. The whole thing is a waste of time. If you want to earn some more money, why don't you get yourself some overtime?"

Muriel brought in the fish and chips, and they all sat down to dine. Andy had laid his anorak over the back of the settee. "And you can put that coat away. I don't want to be eating my tea in a cloakroom." Ted was obviously in a lousy mood, so Andy didn't pursue his request for a sitting. But his father wouldn't let his pet subject drop: "If you want some overtime, why don't you ask Mr Barnthorpe?"

Andy sighed loudly and replaced his knife and fork. "I don't want overtime, Dad, and anyway, there isn't any."

"Well get yourself down to Amiss', the corner shop; they're always advertising for Saturday people.

"They only want schoolchildren, Ted. They don't want anyone over sixteen."

Andy had had enough: "I don't want overtime, Dad. In fact, I don't want to work at Barnthorpe's at all. I want to paint; I'm an artist. I don't want to work in a cotton mill; I want to produce original works of art, to create something."

"By painting that lazy Annie?"

Muriel thought it was time to put a stop to the looming row. "Now, now. Let's hear no ore about it. I don't like arguments, especially at meal times."

The following morning dawned bright and warm, and after a hasty breakfast, Andy started to fuss around with his painting gear. At ten sharp, he was standing talking to Annie. She was sitting on her step, smoking. Andy thought she must be the only woman he knew who would sit for her portrait without having tidied her hair or having changed into her Sunday best. She looked the same today as she always did.

Andy explained: "I'll set up over the road, just outside Mrs Duckinshaw's, that way I'll get a bit of perspective, a little bit of surrounding. This morning, I'll do a few preliminary sketches and maybe a little bit of colour testing, just to get the light and shade right. Would that be all right?"

"Yeh. It's all the same to me."

"You don't have to sit really still or anything, unless I ask you."

As the morning wore on, Andy collected quite a little crowd. Local kids played around his easel and asked him why he wanted to paint and how he managed to make it look so real. One little girl asked some very intelligent questions about observation and translating light and shade onto canvas, and Andy found himself carefully explaining his views and methods. Annie sat impassively staring at the children.

Mrs Duckinshaw and her husband came out of their little house and offered Andy a cup of tea, which he gratefully accepted. "Nice picture that, Andy, lad."

"Well, I've only just started, Mrs Duckinshaw, this is one of my preliminary sketches." He flicked over the pages of his portfolio.

The Duckinshaws looked appreciative. "Very good. It'll cheer Annie up to have her picture done," remarked Mrs Duckinshaw. She waved happily to Annie. Annie waved back. "All right, Annie?"

"Not so bad. How about you?"

"Mustn't grumble." Mr Duckinshaw ruminated: "Why Annie?" Andy launched into his stock explanation. When he had finished, Mr Duckinshaw chuckled. "You'll have to do me and the wife then."

Andy couldn't believe his luck. "If you wouldn't mind, I'd love to. I could do you indoors, say in your parlour, sitting by the fire or maybe looking out of the window. How would that be?"

Mrs Duckinshaw looked at her husband: "Well, what do you think, George?"

"Yeh, why not? See ourselves in oils, eh?"

In his muggy front parlour, Ted called his wife over to him: "What's that daft lad playing at now? Look at him. He's a laughing stock. Go out and tell him to get on in here."

"Leave the boy alone, Ted. He's enjoying himself. Let him be."

In the three weeks that followed, Andy beavered away in his spare time, hardly noticing what was going on around him. As well as finishing Annie's portraits, he was busy in the evenings with his preliminary sketches of the Duckinshaws. Muriel continued to be mildly tolerant of her son's comings and goings, while Ted continued to belittle him. In his euphoria of creativity, Andy hardly noticed.

When he had finished both of the portraits of Annie, Andy went over to see her for the last time. As usual she was sitting on her step, looking out on the world around her. Andy stood over her, partially blocking her view. She seemed not to notice. "I've finished both of the portraits, Annie. Would you like to see them?"

"Yeh. All right then." She looked up at him and he wondered whether she expected him to exhibit the portraits in the street. Did she expect him to go and stand in the middle of the road so she could get the perspective? Apparently not. She slowly stood up. "You'd better come inside then."

For the first and last time, Andy entered Annie's house. He wondered whether she ever had any other visitors to her little front room. It was not unlike his own, except that it was much tidier. The mantelpiece was adorned with a collection of china horses, and there was a cut glass bowl on the small dining table.

"Want a coffee, then?"

"Yes please, if it's not too much trouble."

She lit a cigarette and wandered through into the small kitchen. Andy didn't attempt to follow her.

"There you are then."

"Thanks." Andy noticed she hadn't asked if he took milk or sugar. She took both and assumed everyone else would. "Tell me what you think, then."

He held up the first portrait, the one he intended to show at Jacob Mercer's gallery. He carefully moved the china horses and propped the painting on the mantelshelf. He stood back and looked at it again. Yes. It was all there: the loneliness, the emptiness, the lack of hope. He wondered how Annie would take it.

"Yeh, it's not bad. It looks like me. Yeh. I like it."

"So do I. I'm pleased with it. In some ways I think it's the best thing I've ever done. You were a good model." Andy trotted over to the mantelpiece and changed over the portraits. "This is your one. It's like the other one, but it's a bit different. Do you like it?" It was a softer portrayal than the first, gentler, with more sunlight falling on her face.

"Yeh. Thanks. I like it fine. It's good. Hang it up. Where that picture of the Chinese girl is."

"Can I stand on one of your dining chairs?" In a very few minutes Annie's portrait was installed on the wall over the television set. Andy carefully replaced the collection of china horses and said good-bye. Annie followed him out of the front door and returned to her step.

Jacob Mercer was very impressed by Andy's final portfolio.

"Wonderful, Andy. Simply wonderful. I knew you could do it. That sunset is divine. Marvellous. And that girl, the one on the step. Oh yes, here it is. "Watching the World Go By". Appropriate title. Where did you find her?"

"She lives near me. She's always sitting on her step. She doesn't work; she doesn't seem to do anything. She just sits there, day after day, looking out over the street."

"It's the best thing you've done. Those eyes. So hopeless."

Andy was fortunate enough to catch the public mood with his first exhibition and he obtained unexpectedly good prices for his canvases. Equally importantly, he also obtained a number of excellent reviews in the local and national press and culture magazines. The portrait of Annie was singled out for particular praise and a certain amount of interest was expressed in the model herself. Believing it to be in her best interests, Andy never disclosed her identity; he thought her physical and mental states wouldn't stand too much probing. Fortunately, this interest soon subsided, and the *cognoscenti* continued to admire and chatter and, occasionally, to buy.

Unfortunately, Andy's public success was more than matched by the deterioration of his home circumstances. His father became increasingly short of breath and temper, and even the commercial success of his son's artwork cut little ice.

"And now what are you going to do, eh? You've sold all them pictures, and about time too, though God knows why anyone would want to buy them, but what are you going to do now? Your mother and me could do with a few more bob coming in every week."

"Oh, Ted, Andy always pays his way. I've no complaints. He's always been good to us."

"Now I'm launched as an artist, I'll be able to sell more paintings, as and then I do them. I'll be able to give up Barnthorpe's."

Ted spluttered. "What! You give up Barnthorpe's. What for? You've got a damned good job down there. Don't you go giving it up. Not if you want to go on living in this house."

Muriel gave her son a knowing look; she'd had a little chat with him while Ted had been down the Dog and Whistle. "Well, that's the thing, Dad. I won't be living here much longer. I've decided to get a flat in Manchester, so I'll be able to paint full-time."

Ted was beside himself. He expected his son and heir to support him, at least until he got married. He most certainly did not expect him to move out of the district and set up on his own. "That's just like you. Get a few bob in your pocket and you're off, never mind your mother and me." Ted's coughing became uncontrollable.

Muriel attempted to comfort him: "Now, now, dear. He's got to leave home sometime. He's got to make his own way in the world. We won't be here for ever and neither will Barnthorpe's. They've been losing money for years now; there's no future in factory work these days."

Sitting sketching in his flat five years later, Andy looked back on his mother's words and thought she had shown a great deal of percipience. Shortly after he had moved to Manchester, Barnthorpe's had closed their doors for the last time and made the remaining three hundred workers, including Paul and Mark, redundant. One year later, exhausted by caring for her husband, Muriel had quietly died. It was one of the continuing regrets of Andy's life that he had never painted her.

Despite predictions to the contrary, Ted had continued to struggle on for a further two years. At one stage he had been admitted to the Royal Infirmary with suspected cirrhosis of the liver. An operation was ruled out of the question: Ted's lungs were in no condition to withstand an anaesthetic process. His doctors sent him home with a strong recommendation to stay away from the booze. Following his wife's death, Ted had made Andy's life a misery with his continual requests to come and live with his son. When he was no longer able to visit the pub, he had made his son's life hell. Andy had firmly withstood the pressure and had arranged for the social services to look after his father. He had even paid for a home help, and would have paid for Ted to live in an old people's residential home, rather than be subject to the pressure of living with him again. However, Ted had died before that decision had become necessary.

After his father's death, Andy's paintings had continued to enjoy a vogue and his portraits, in particular, became much in demand. Heads of industry and new lords queued up to be immortalized. For his part, Andy was more than happy to paint the rich or famous, or in some cases their stately homes, if it provided sufficient money for him to be able to continue to capture his fellow citizens and their environs on canvas.

From time to time his thoughts wandered back to Annie. Did she still sit on her step, smoking, looking out on the world with those hopeless eyes? Was that wraith-like figure still the eternal spectator?

One Saturday Andy was invited to give a lecture at the New Arts Gallery in Rossdale and, after his talk, he found himself alone in his old town. Suddenly he had the urge to see Annie again, to paint her again. He ambled slowly through the main market square in the direction of Dodgson Street. As he remembered it, the market had always been full of colour and life, even late in the mornings, but now it appeared dull and lifeless, the stalls tawdry and irrelevant. It started to rain and Andy pulled his coat collar up to shield his face from the sleeting droplets.

When he reached Dodgson Street, he looked up at his old house. It was much as he remembered. He crossed over the corner. He almost expected to see her sitting on her step, even in the rain, but she wasn't there. Andy strolled over and knocked on the door. There was no reply; the house was completely silent and obviously empty. He stood back and looked up at the windows. Annie had bought herself come new curtains. He was surprised she was out, but presumably she did have to go out sometime.

As he turned to go, Andy saw Mr Duckinshaw looking out of his window. The front door opened and Mrs Duckinshaw called out: "How are you, lad?"

Andy strolled over: "Fine, thanks. How about you?"

"Still waiting for the council to re-house us." Mr Duckinshaw had joined his wife on the step. "We can't cope here any more. We'd like a nice little flat, so we wouldn't have to do the garden, but the council haven't got anything."

"Oh, I'm sorry. I suppose there's no chance of being able to buy anything? I notice prices have dropped a lot round here. I guess it's on account of there being no work."

Mrs Duckinshaw looked at her husband. "That would be the ideal, naturally, so we could leave it to Rita when we're gone, then she would always have a little place of her own. We even talked about it, and she said she could help us out a bit, but, even with our little bit of savings, we still wouldn't have enough."

"Oh, that's a shame."

"Are you still doing the paintings, lad?"

"Yes. Those portraits I did of you and Annie really did well for me. People are queuing up to have their portraits painted."

"Good, lad. We're only too pleased. Aren't we, Grace? Was it Annie you were wanting to see?"

"Yes, but it looks as though she's out."

Grace looked uneasily at George and he looked at Andy. "Ah well, lad, you won't be seeing her any more. None of us will. She's dead, lad. God rest her soul."

Andy gasped: "Oh no. I'd no idea. What happened? I didn't know she was ill."

Grace looked even more uneasy: "She killed herself, son. Hanged herself from the bannisters." Andy's heart sank. He had so wanted to see Annie again.

"Come in and have a cup of tea, Andy."

As soon as he entered the familiar parlour, he saw his

portrait, the one he had given to Annie, hanging over the fireplace.

While his wife made tea, George explained: "After she hanged herself, the council came round to clear her place out, on account of Annie having no family. We saw them and said they should give that there painting to your dad. We thought he should have it, on account of it being yours."

Grace returned with the tea: "We didn't know where you were, lad, otherwise we'd have written and told you." She looked embarrassed. Andy couldn't understand why.

He asked: "And when dad died, you got it?"

George shifted uneasily. "Not exactly, lad. To be honest, your dad didn't want it. He said it weren't worth nothing and he didn't care for it."

"I'm sorry, lad." Grace patted Andy's knee. "But we like it, don't we, George? It reminds us of young Annie."

Andy had an idea: "If you wanted to sell it, I reckon you could get quite a few thousand; it might help you out, if you found a little flat you wanted. Look, I'll give you my phone number, and if you do decide to sell, I'll put you in touch with the right people, someone who'll give you a fair price, a gallery, where you could visit her."

"That would be grand, lad. What do you think, dear?"

Mrs Duckinshaw agreed, and patted Andy on the shoulder. She knew he had given them a most precious gift.

They all looked up at the portrait. Annie was still sitting on her step, looking down at them, watching the world go by.

GERTRAUDE

The rain was pouring down as Ted miserably looked through the window of his portable cabin office. He sighed. Although it was January, the weather was not all that cold, which was just as well, considering that the heating did not work and there was a hole in the ceiling. As Ted regarded the downpour a piece of guttering fell off and hit the window. He could only hope the carpet in the seminar room would be dried out in time for the first speaker. That, at least, was one problem off his mind: Professor Braun had promised to get the new guest-lecturer programme off to a flying start, and he was going to be cheap too. He was already in the country for a cooperative project in Warwick, so they would not have to pay his air fares. All that remained was to fill the other five slots. Mifsud had promised to come over from Liverpool if they should need him. He always did and most years they did. He was a former student of the department who had done well for himself by a combination of ruthless flattery and talking about his work to anyone who would listen, but, thought Ted irritably, that did nothing to improve the quality of his science.

Charles bounced into the room, spraying rain over Ted's papers. "How're you getting on? It's raining cats and dogs out there."

"The usual troubles: we're a small department with a middle of the road reputation; the big names don't think it's a good way to use their time."

Charles helped himself to the last hot coffee in Ted's flask. "What about Angelika Schmidt, from Vienna?"

Ted was wary. Charles was a band-wagon-jumper, and in the past some of his enthusiasms had been bizarre. "As always, Charles, it's a question of cost. Isn't she that woman who spent two years in the Australian outback, sampling every species of salt-bush and mangrove she could lay her hands on, only to be told by the journal she submitted the report to that one sample from each was not enough? It was laughable, or would have been, had it not represented such a waste of research funding. I don't think she would be good value for money."

Charles was puzzled. "I know I haven't seen her publication yet, but I assumed she was too busy to get round to it. I didn't know it had been bounced. How did you know?"

"I was one of the referees who bounced it. Twice in fact: once from Natural Environment and once from the Accounts of Botany."

Charles was crestfallen. "They didn't ask me to give my opinion. I must say I've always found her work rather good."

Ted smelled a rat. Charles's opinions of the work of his female colleagues were notoriously eccentric and often depended on his feelings for them as females rather than as scientists. If this was the case, Ted had no intention of gratifying Charles's lusts by inviting a putative girlfriend for an all-expenses-paid trip to meet Charles. "That effort was risible; she showed not the slightest indication of statistical method; she didn't even take precautions over the storage and preservation of her samples prior to analysis. And I don't remember anything else that she's done that has been particularly good."

"Well you can bear her in mind if you're stuck. She'd be a better choice than Mifsud. If I have to listen to another of his badly planned, badly executed, wrongly concluded crusades, I'll puke."

In due time Professor Braun honoured Ted's department with his presence and proved to be remarkably good value. He was taken out to dine in the evening and, much to Ted's surprise, praised Angelika Schmidt most warmly. "An excellent young worker. Her research in Freiburg has been of the first class. When they sent me their preliminary report, I was most happy. It should come out in Natural Environment this month."

Charles looked at Ted. Ted shrugged; he had not been asked to review that one. "What has she been doing in Freiburg, then?"

"They have been making investigations into forest death, on a government contract."

Ted almost groaned. He should have known: that type of political contract, relying, as it doubtless did, on simple observation combined with massive, badly constructed field trials, would be right up Dr Schmidt's strasse.

"They have been examining some of the structures of the vessels when the trees are exposed to SO_2. Angelika has made some very good observations. I may have a pre-publication copy here with me. I shall give it to you."

Charles beamed. Ted forced summer pudding into his mouth.

The professor was as good as his word and the next day Ted had to admit that, if this really was Schmidt's work, she had improved considerably since her days in Australia. Charles also read the publication. "There you are, Ted. I said she'd be good valuc, didn't I?"

"Who is this Petra Amiel, do you know?"

Charles shook his head. "Not a clue. Why?"

"Just a thought." After Charles had left his office Ted cautiously dialled the phone number given in the address at the head of the paper. After considerable wrangling with the German telephone system and the university's own switchboard, he was finally connected to Professorin Amiel. She sounded elderly and her English was poor. He politely mentioned that his department was in a similar line of work to hers, and that he was very interested in the work she had been doing with Angelika Schmidt.

"But naturally, Professor Clayman, that is the work of Doktorin Schmidt. My own interest are in senescence." Professorin Amiel pronounced all the consonants. "My input in this is very small."

Ted knew that it was the custom in many European institutes for the professor to give formal permission for the submission of a publication, and that they often ended up named as an author when they had not contributed to the actual research.

Professorin Amiel was continuing: "But you cannot speak with her now. She is not here. She is in your own country, in London, in the Walbrook College with Professor Cartier. You may call to her there."

Ted thanked Professorin Amiel and thought that his luck was in. If Angelika Schmidt had written that publication alone, she would have been worth the flight from Freiburg, but now she would only cost the return rail from London. He resolved to contact her at once.

Later that week he was able to inform his colleagues that they would not have to endure Mifsud again this year: "I've invited Angelika Schmidt up from London to entertain us."

Charles looked radiant.

Even Fergus smiled: "Entertain is about the right word, I should say. I remember her from that conference in Spain a couple of years ago. She was quite something. Stunning, in fact. Lovely hair, that Teutonic blonde, you know, but wavy. And a great figure. Is she any good?"

"Her latest publication is very good. She's done some pretty ropey stuff in the past, but maybe this structural work is her forte. Professor Braun spoke very highly of her when he was here."

"That's no surprise. They spent most of that week in Spain glued together like two leeches." Fergus sounded jealous.

Ted was smelling the rat again. "Charles, you were at Bilbao, weren't you?"

"Sure. It was the first I'd ever seen or heard of her. But I could not get a look in. Still, where there's life, there's hope, eh?"

Ted's hope was fading fast until he remembered that Dr Schmidt had also been recommended by Professor Amiel, and she was a woman.

Two weeks passed before the department was saddened to learn that Professor Braun had died. To round off his successful tour of the UK he had gone to London and treated himself to some days sightseeing, expressing the hope to meet up with Angelika. Some kind soul had nipped up behind him in an underpass by the South Bank and belted him several times over the head with a length of lead piping. His camera was missing.

"I wonder if Angelika Schmidt knows," asked Fergus. "They may not be an item now, but they must have been pretty close once. I bet she'll be upset."

Ted sighed and rooted out Mifsud's number, just in case. He managed to contact Angelika at Walbrook College and was relieved to hear her firm-voiced reassurance: "But no, Professor Clayman, I am in control of myself, although I had actually heard the sad news only yesterday. There is no problem at all. You may be sure I will come for your meeting."

As the date of Dr Schmidt's seminar approached, Charles became increasingly happy at the thought of seeing her again. Even Fergus smartened himself up. Ted was intrigued: whatever Angelika's scientific qualities, she certainly radiated an effect on his staff.

It was then that Charles' pursuit of beauty reached too far. The seminar was scheduled for Tuesday afternoon, with a tour of the department and discussions with students and other members of staff to occupy the rest of the day. Charles reasoned that since Angelika would lose Monday to travelling anyway, it would be more civilized and less tiring for her to journey on the Saturday and enjoy a couple of days seeing the city in the company of a friendly guide, who could also be relied upon to provide accommodation. Knowing Ted's suspicious mind, Charles did not bother to tell him that he was going to hijack the department's guest, and he did not mention it to Fergus, in order to avoid competition.

Angelika was at first guarded: "Your offer, Doktor Walsh, is most kindly, but it is hardly correct, since we do not know each other."

"But we do. We met in Spain, in Bilbao, at the conference dinner. I was sitting across the table from you and poor Braun."

"Of course, I remember you. I am so sorry I did not recall your name now." The reply sounded like a sigh.

Charles thought she did not sound too enthusiastic, but then she seemed to make up her mind: "So, in that case, Doktor Walsh, I must thank you for your kind offer, and I shall look forward to meeting also Frau Walsh on Saturday."

At this point Charles found it expedient not to mention that Frau Walsh had left him several years ago. Instead, he arranged to meet the train arriving from London at 2.15 p.m. He was whistling a happy tune as he passed Fergus on the way to the labs.

Fergus bumped into Ted: "Charles is a happy man all of a sudden. I wonder what he's up to?"

Ted thought he might have an idea, but no amount of hinting throughout the rest of the week could persuade Charles to confess the secret of his contentment.

Charles was still ridiculously cheerful as he groomed himself to meet the London train that Saturday, but his happiness was short-lived.

Just how short became clear when, after he failed to report for work on Monday morning, Ted phoned him at home. Receiving no reply, Ted worried throughout the morning and finally resolved to visit Charles's flat during the lunch hour. As he drove through the town the ignoble thought that Charles might have run off with the beautiful Angelika occurred to him.

Arriving at the flat, Ted was admitted by a young man whom he did not know. An older man introduced himself as a police inspector and started to question him about Charles, who had been found battered to death in his own lounge. A workman, who had been given a key by the letting agent, had made the discovery that morning, and was still sitting hunched up in an armchair. Charles had obviously been murdered where he had been found and had been dead for just under two days. In addition to asking Ted about Charles's life and work within the department, the police also established that Ted had an excellent alibi for the whole of Saturday, before releasing him with the caution that they would be visiting his department as soon as they had finished at the flat.

Although the police were inclined to believe that Charles had been murdered by a friend, probably female, rather than by a work colleague, they were extremely thorough in their enquiries, and Ted's department was much disturbed for the whole of Monday afternoon and much of the evening. The only glimmer of a lead came from Fergus's mention of Charles's state of mind during the preceding week.

The Tuesday dawned cold and grey, and Ted was thoroughly miserable as he pulled into the car park. He walked in with Fergus: "Rum do that. Poor old Charles. I wonder if the police will be in again today."

"I doubt it; when I locked up last night they didn't indicate that they would. It's unbelievable. It still hasn't sunk in. Who would do such a thing?"

Fergus held open the door. "Well, you know Charles. I suppose it's a case of *cherchez la femme*."

Ted looked sadly at Fergus. "A woman could have done it, certainly. Whoever it was just kept battering until he was dead."

"Talking of women, when are we expecting the lovely Dr Schmidt?"

"Oh my God." Ted wiped his hand over his face. "I'd completely forgotten about that. I suppose it's too late to cancel her now. She was going to travel up yesterday; I'd booked her into the Regency. I wonder if she knows?"

"Only if she's seen a local paper or the TV news last night. They did a nice panorama of the campus on the news."

A porter stepped up to Ted: "Professor, there was a phone call for you at about half-eight this morning. A foreign lady, a Doctor Smith, said she would not now be able to attend your meeting today."

"Thank you. Did she leave a contact number?"

"Nah. She rang off sharpish. Said she had to go."

When Ted contacted the Regency Hotel, it transpired that his guest had never checked in. Before he could examine the significance of Angelika's absence, the police arrived, bearing video equipment and a tape taken from the Railway Station's CCTV. They explained that in response to the previous evening's TV appeal, a neighbour of Charles had come forward to report that he had seen him at about twenty past two on the afternoon of the previous Saturday, meeting a mousey-looking woman off the London train. This was confirmed by the video footage, which Ted and his colleagues were required to view in an attempt to identify the woman. No one could, but the police were interested to learn that Dr Schmidt had absented herself.

"Could this be her?" they asked.

"Definitely not. I met her at a conference a few years ago and she looked nothing like that. Angelika Schmidt is a very beautiful woman." Something in the inspector's look embarrassed Fergus. "No, not me. Charles had his eye on her, but she was with Professor Braun."

Ted was pensive. "And Braun was battered to death in London a couple of weeks ago, when Angelika Schmidt was working there and could easily have arranged to meet him. And it would have been just like Charles to invite our beautiful guest for a weekend prior to her visit to the department."

At this stage the police were beginning to look very interested: "You think, Professor, that instead of the expected beauty, Dr Walsh was greeted by an altogether more deadly lady, armed, no doubt, with a very plausible excuse as to why she was standing in for Angelika Schmidt."

Ted nodded. "More deadly and, I think, a far better scientist."

"Whoever she is, this woman is the last person we can find to see your colleague alive. We'll try to trace that phone call and get on to the ports and airports, but if your theory is correct, she'll be long gone by now and cleaning out Dr Schmidt's assets before changing identity. She's probably realized by now how difficult it would be to maintain that role. How many more people would she come across who could identify the real Dr Schmidt?"

Fergus caught on. "Poor Charles. Poor Braun."

"And poor, silly Angelika. You'll never find her, inspector: she's buried in an Australian mangrove swamp."

A WORK OF ART

Arnold sat patiently beside Trevor as they watched Mrs Armstrong shuffle her papers. The scent of sweet peas drifted in from the immaculate garden. Trevor turned and watched the cloud shadows scurry across the broad lawn. How on earth did someone so decrepit manage to keep this place going?

Mrs Armstrong looked up from her papers. "My eldest boy does the garden."

"It's beautiful." Arnold, at least, was genuinely appreciative. He was a keen gardener himself. "Are those Old-English roses by the gate?"

"Yes, Mr Hemingway, Frank planted them the year he died, so I'm very fond of them."

"Can I help you with that?" Trevor leaned forward.

Mrs Armstrong pulled her papers back across the coffee table. "No thank you; some of them are personal."

"If we are to do a proper job for you, we need to have an accurate estimate of how you stand."

"With difficulty." Mrs Armstrong nodded towards her Zimmer Frame. "Here we are." Mrs Armstrong changed spectacles. "Now, what was it you wanted to know?"

Arnold took the lead. "I understand that you're worried about inheritance tax, Mrs Armstrong. You want to make sure your son and daughter don't have to worry." That was about as tactful a way as he knew of describing the great unmentionable.

"After I'm dead, you mean?"

Mrs Armstrong enjoyed discussing the prospect of her own demise, so it was over an hour before Arnold and Trevor were ready to leave, armed with an extensive list of Mrs Armstrong's assets. Trevor reckoned that after the happy event Henry and Julia would never need to worry again, unless they counted the prospect of disposing of half a mill. as a worry.

On the way through the dining room Trevor's eye was caught by a hideous painting which occupied most of the chimney breast. He joked to Arnold: "She's got it upside-down."

Mrs Armstrong's ears were better than her legs. "No I haven't. It's abstract. It explores spatial relationships and tonal qualities."

Arnold shot Trevor a black look. "It's very striking. Particularly the blue; very unusual."

Trevor scrutinized the work more closely. "Is that a leg sticking out of the ear there?"

"It's not an ear. But I'm glad *you* appreciate it, Mr Hemmingway. It's not one of his best works, but I've always had a soft spot for it. He was such a dear. I've got it well insured."

"Very wise, Mrs Armstrong. Well, I'll be back in a fortnight. Wednesday at two, and then we can discuss a few ideas, see what you think. In the meantime, if there's anything you think of, don't hesitate to give me a call."

Back in the car, Trevor lit up. "What a bore. Still, she was worth it. I wonder where she got all that money from? Her old man was only a perfume salesman."

"Put that out. You know they make me cough, and if my wife smells smoke in the car, I'll never hear the last of it. And it doesn't matter how Mrs Armstrong got her money, she's got it now, and I've got to do my best to see that her family gets to hold on to it."

Arnold started the car. "And by the way, I'm going to ask Roger to assign you to another trainer, I shan't be taking you back to Mrs Armstrong or to any more of my clients. You can get your percentage on the ones we've already completed, but that's it."

"Thanks for nothing. I don't need you anyway."

"As far as I can tell from your commissions, you need all the help you can get. I don't know how you keep going on what you earn."

"Mind your own."

"I'm only trying to help. Look, in this business you've got to treat the customer well, be respectful to them. If I noticed you yawning, I'm sure Mrs Armstrong did too, and why did you have to make that snide remark about the painting?"

"Because it was cack: blue legs sticking out of a head. Worth a bit, though, I suppose."

When Arnold returned two weeks later, it was to a very subdued Mrs Armstrong. She led him through the dining room and into the lounge. The weather was still fine, but the windows and patio door were shut fast and the house was silent, very different from his first visit. Arnold lowered himself onto the sofa and looked about him.

Mrs Armstrong sat opposite and twisted a moist handkerchief in her hands. "I'm sorry, Mr Hemmingway; I should not have let you come. I should have telephoned, but I thought I'd be all right."

"Oh dear, Mrs Armstrong, whatever is the matter? If I've come at a bad time, we can always make another appointment." Arnold reached for his office diary.

"Thank you. I'm sorry to have wasted your time, but since the burglary, I don't know where I am."

Arnold was stunned, and then he realized what was different about his surroundings: the trinkets were gone. The carriage clock no longer ticked on the mantelpiece; the crystal and silver no longer gleamed from the display cabinet, and there were no photographs twinkling in silver frames.

"I'm so sorry. How awful for you. Did they get much?"

"Everything that was valuable and portable. Thank Heavens, I've never kept much money in the house, apart from a few pounds."

"What about bank cards and that sort of thing?"

"I don't use them. As you know, most of my spare money is in the building society. My next-door neighbour kindly drove me straight down to the branch in Ferring so I could let them know my pass-book had been stolen. They were very kind, and it was all taken care of before the thief had the opportunity to make any withdrawals. And you mustn't worry: I've still got all my policies and share documents. I suppose they couldn't do anything with them, so they left them alone."

Arnold quickly checked through Mrs Armstrong's list of holdings: shares held in the electronic register, insurances, and long-term investments, which could not be withdrawn early. "I think you're right, Mrs Armstrong, as long as you're sure absolutely everything is here."

"Oh yes. I checked most carefully when I made the list out for the police. As for the rest, they weren't very hopeful. They said the good stuff would have been sold to dishonest antique dealers in Brighton. It's heartbreaking; although most of it wasn't particularly valuable, it had sentimental value. My photographs are all gone, and they're irreplaceable: I haven't got copies of most of them, and the negatives deteriorated years ago. And the carriage clock was given to Frank when he retired, and they took my lovely painting…" She began to cry.

Arnold consoled her.

On his way home he thought about Mrs Armstrong. She was a tough old girl, but a thing like that could be shattering at her age. He felt very sorry for her, but she was not alone. To his certain knowledge there had been at least half a dozen similar robberies within the past couple of months. They had been reported in the local press, and the police had warned the elderly and vulnerable to be careful when strangers came to call. They opined that the burglars had taken great care in selecting their victims, and it had come as no surprise to Arnold that Mrs Entwhistle, a disabled lady of some fifty years, had told him and Trevor a similar story one spring afternoon when they had called back with her savings plan application, or that Mr Hughes, a retired banker, had lost his collection of Japanese art and had been too distracted to consider their investment proposals. Arnold made a mental note to call them both and enquire about their current well-being.

Arnold drove through the old part of town. It would be Jacqui's eighteenth in a couple of months, and he knew she had a liking for antique jewellery. For several weeks now he had been scouring the antiques quarter in the hope of finding something to delight. Walking down Old Passage, he saw Trevor emerge from the Latimer Gallery. Mildly interested, since he had never thought of Trevor as a culture-lover, he wandered over to peer in the window. It was much as he had expected: fake sentimental Victorian paintings, etchings of dubious artistic merit, and small oils by the long dead and unremembered jostled for public admiration.

Inside the shop he could see the owner examining a new acquisition. He rang the bell and was admitted. "May I just browse?" Trying to appear casual, he wandered round the gallery, the elderly owner's eyes wandering with him.

"What kind of thing were you looking for?"

Arnold lied: "Something abstract, a bit modern. It's my daughter's coming of age soon and she likes paintings."

"We don't get much of that kind of thing: we don't have a market for it. I doubt that you'll find anything like that round here. Why not get her a bit of jewellery? Girls like that."

If Arnold had not been suspicious before, he was now. The idea of an antique dealer sending a customer elsewhere was unbelievable. "What about that? It looks fun. May I have a look? Could you put it on the easel?"

"It's not for sale." Arnold and the antique dealer stood on either side of the painting, eyeing one another.

He had made the old boy suspicious. If he left now, Mrs Armstrong would never get the painting back. There was only one thing to do: he grabbed the painting and held on to it.

"What's your game, friend? Don't get funny with me, or I'll call the law."

"By all means do, Mr Latimer. I'll wait here with this painting until they come. I'm sure they'll be only too happy to return it to its legal owner."

"Don't you give me that, chum. That was a legitimate purchase. I paid twenty quid for it."

"So you will have no difficulty in divulging who sold it to you, and how they came by it."

Mr Latimer's profit instinct fought with his desire to avoid internment. It was just his luck to be alone in the shop. Twenty years ago, before the bypasses, he could have shown this joker the door. But not now.

Arnold struggled to manipulate his mobile out of his pocket, while still hugging the painting. "Police, please…"

"All right, all right. Seeing as you like it so much, it's yours for fifty."

"Yes, I'd like to report…"

"Yeah. Give me my twenty. And clear off."

Arnold was glad to oblige. Feeling as guilty as if he had stolen the painting himself, he scurried back to his car, and turned once more towards Mrs Armstrong's house. At least he now knew how Trevor managed to keep body and soul together. An anonymous tip to Crimestoppers should soon sever that connection.

Half an hour later, Arnold, artwork in tow, was back with Mrs Armstrong. She was almost incoherent with joy. "My beautiful portrait. Wherever did you find it?"

Arnold tactfully explained. He supposed he had compounded a felony, but Mrs Armstrong had no such scruples, and gratefully reimbursed him.

"It was so clever of you, Mr Hemmingway, to buy it back for only £20. I'm sure Pablo would be very aggrieved if he knew."

"Pablo?"

"Picasso, Mr Hemmingway. He could be such a dear when he chose." Registering the astonishment on Arnold's face, she explained: "We met him when Frank was working for Chanel in the south of France. Of course, I had no idea when I posed for him that he would give me this one."

Looking at Mrs Armstrong clutching her Zimmer Frame, Arnold could not bring himself to ask how she had ever managed to contort herself into that position. "You mean that the… er… thief and that gallery owner have both parted with a genuine Picasso for the princely sum of £20?"

Mrs Armstrong chuckled. "Yes indeed, Mr Hemmingway. Unlike you, they have no souls."

BOBBY AND GILBERT

"What number did you say it was?"

"Number twenty-three ; over there. He said it was next to the allotments."

Sean parked his Nova across the road and cast a professional eye over the property. "Not much money there, by the look of it. How old did you say they were?"

"I didn't ask, but he said they were pensioners."

Sean was adjusting his tie and sliding a comb through his gel. "Oh God. Do tell me you bothered to find out whether they've got anything worth talking about."

"Gilbert said he wanted to discuss their savings, so I suppose they must have some." Denny was beginning to regret the decision to bring her line manager along, but her sales had been so desperate of late, she had to do something to avoid the axe.

"Right, let's get it over with; and smarten yourself up. Wear a suit next time. Didn't they tell you that in training? Or can't you afford one? What a dump."

The bungalow did, indeed, look far from inspiring. The front lawns on either side of the concrete path were reasonably kept, but the paint-work was peeling and the bell did not work. However, Gilbert must have been watching out for them; in a surprisingly short time he was showing them into the dingy hall. "Miss Abbott?"

"Yes; pleased to meet you. This is my manager, Mr O'Brien. He's one of our investment specialists, so I thought it might be a good idea to bring him along, if that's all right with you."

Gilbert shook hands with Denny and cast an unfavourable eye over the spiv while ushering them into the rear lounge.

Denny gasped. It was like stepping into a tropical rainforest. Greenery of large and unidentifiable forms issued from the walls, trailed along the old-fashioned picture rail, and sprouted from the Axminster. The foliage was so dense that it was difficult to discern its containers. Sean collided with a large earthen-ware urn, and purply-red pollen showered on to the carpet and over his shoulders. Gilbert gave the plant an affectionate pat on the stalk and ignored Sean. "Please do sit on the sofa, there, opposite the picture window."

Denny and Sean sat side by side. As her eyes became accustomed to the light she saw a figure spread into one of the matching armchairs, a tanned, smiling figure, whom Gilbert introduced as his wife, Bobby.

"Sean O'Brien, investment consultant; my card."

Bobby nodded and, in a remarkably high-pitched voice, asked: "And who is your offsider, Mr O'Brien?"

Denny caught on. "Denise Abbott, Mrs Parkin."

"Would you care for some tea, Miss Abbott?"

"Thank you. That would be very nice."

Sean surreptitiously looked at his watch. At this rate they would be lucky to get away before closing time. He leaned back on the sofa and caused a spidery weed to catch the crown of his head. He jumped. Denny helped him to brush it away.

"Lovely, isn't it, Miss Abbott? It's one of my favourites. Parasitic, you know."

"What?" This time Sean made it off the sofa.

"On other plants, Mr O'Brien."

Denny was beginning to like Bobby more by the minute. She looked carefully around the room. Mixed in with the foliage was a collection of wooden sculptures and wall decorations. They were like nothing she had ever seen before.

Bobby's eyes followed hers. "The Maori call it a mere, Miss Abbott. It's a club. This one is for ceremonial use, not for everyday."

Gilbert returned with the best china and cherry cake. Denny thought that Bobby was probably too fat to bend over the coffee table. "Home-made," he offered. "I've made a list of our savings, all typed out ready for you." He handed the paper to Denny.

Sean dumped his empty cup on the table and grasped the typed sheet. Now he too was beginning to like Bobby more by the minute. "Thank you. I think that's all very clear, Mr Parkin. Is everything here?"

Gilbert nodded. From Denny's brief glimpse, she had concluded there was more than enough. She opened her briefcase and extracted the financial planning questionnaire. Before she had managed to complete their names and address, Sean was in full flow. "Well, these UTs are well out of order, and these insurances, I ask you. With the amount you've got here, you should be going for something a lot more profitable."

Denny gasped. Bobby smiled on. Gilbert asked: "What do you think, Miss Abbott?"

"Perhaps we'd better do a little bit of paper-work and discuss what it is you want your savings to do for you." She pulled the paper away from Sean.

He muttered something which sounded like: "They want to get rich, what do you think?" He looked at his watch again.

"I think, Miss Abbott, that your colleague is in a hurry to be away. Perhaps we should detain you no longer, Mr O'Brien." Gilbert rose and indicated the door.

Sean used it reluctantly. Without Denny he could have had the whole lot wrapped up in half an hour, but now he was going to have to go through the pantomime of planning and paying them a second visit before he could fill in his commission docket. He put on his amiable face. "Thank you, sir; I'm afraid my schedule is always tight. Miss Abbott can take all your details and I promise to give them my full attention tomorrow."

Denny heard the car draw away. She would have to walk back to the office. Returning to her paper-work, it occurred to her that "Bobby" was probably not Mrs Parkin's legal name.

"I'll spell it for you." Denny followed instructions. "It's a Pacific Island name. That's where I come from. Where I met my prince." Bobby smiled lovingly at the returned Gilbert.

"And where I married the King's Daughter." He kissed Bobby on the head. He disappeared into the jungle and returned with an old brown photograph in a wooden frame.

Superficially, Denny could see that it was like the long school photographs she had had taken in her childhood: two long rows of artificially smiling faces dressed in their finery and seated one behind the other. However, these faces featured more adults than children. Some of them wore cloth, but the majority wore only grass skirts, and some very little at all, if one discounted nose-bones and tooth necklaces. Gilbert pointed out Bobby and her father, who was the central figure in this little community of the long ago. Bobby was seated with a group of other females, and it was impossible to recognize the Mrs Parkin of today in that svelte, coy maiden.

"Gilbert took that photograph, Miss Abbott. It was the first time any of us had seen a camera. Father wasn't too keen on the idea at first: he thought that our souls would all be captured into the box."

"But I persuaded him by telling him that I would give him the picture afterwards, so he would be the owner of everything in it. He didn't understand that I would have the negative. I had to develop it at the dead of night. I hate to think what he would have done if he had found out. As it was, he took it as important homage, a sort of smoothing of the path." He smiled at Bobby.

"How did you come to be in the Pacific, Mr Parkin?"

"In those days I was young and adventurous. I came from a poor family in Chatham, so the sea was always part of our life. After I left school at the age of fourteen, I became a deck-boy on a tramp, and then one thing led to another, and I drifted ever eastwards until I ended up in the islands in the early thirties. There was nothing for me at home apart from the depression and the damp, so I stayed on. Slice of cherry cake, Miss Abbott?"

Looking at the frail Gilbert now, it was impossible for Denny to imagine this master of the sponge cake sailing round the world, braving storms and the unknown. "Thank you, please call me Denny."

Bobby smiled and nodded at Gilbert. Gilbert smiled timidly at Denny.

Denny studied the photograph more closely, searching for the subject of an intelligent question. Bobby nodded again. "That's right, Denny, those are human bones. All my ancestors had been cannibals, until the missionaries arrived, of course." Gilbert chuckled. "Some of those artefacts were two hundred years old."

Denny found herself entirely on the side of the missionaries, but Gilbert pointed out: "Eating captives gave you their power, like owning their likenesses or tribal totems, of course, but it was also a very necessary source of protein."

"As an alternative to fish," explained Bobby.

"It may be shocking to the modern mind, but it was by no means uncommon in the Far East in those days." Gilbert finished his tea. "When the Australians started sending out teams of jungle fighters against the Japs in the Second World War, they went out and recruited amongst the islanders because they were such good warriors, and used to the conditions. They didn't give them much choice and, being a European able to speak both sets of languages, they made me a sergeant. I'll never forget Captain Chambers' face when he found out how his company had kept so fit through it all." He chuckled and Bobby joined in.

"So, how did you get on with the old dears last night?"

"They were fascinating; he's had an amazing life, and she's…"

"Yeh, yeh. Did you get a sale?"

"No. I didn't try to. They've got about 350 thousand spare, and it's going to take a bit of sorting out."

"Three hundred and fifty grand, and they live like that. Christ. What do they do with it all?"

"They have a lot of dependants: twelve children, all adults, some living here, and some in New Zealand, and a few in the islands. But they haven't lived in this country for most of their lives, and they've never paid NI, so they don't get a pension and they have to live off their savings. Not only that, but they want to help their grandchildren go to college or set themselves up in business, and that's not cheap."

Sean was flicking through the paper-work. He was not a fan of education. In his opinion it did not pay to have too much. "What's this? They're already with Carpenter's, the independent guy in Dunsford."

"Gilbert explained that. They had been recommended to them by a neighbour, but they soon became disenchanted with the length of time it took for their investments to come through. I don't understand why it took him so long. We can get that kind of new business through in under a fortnight."

Sean carefully replaced his gold fountain pen on his leather blotter. "Work it out for yourself. What's the interest on 350K for four months? One way and another, he did pretty well out of those suckers; but he spoiled it by getting too greedy, and now he's lost them. So, we'll have to be a bit careful."

"Oh no. Absolutely not, Sean. That's fraud, and I won't have anything to do with it. They're nice old people."

"OK. It was just a suggestion. You get on with those pension opt-outs that came in yesterday, and I'll get on with sorting this out."

"I told them I'd go back next week with a plan of action."

Sean understood her, but he had no intention of losing the Parkins or sharing them with Denny. All he had to do was swap their current investments for something producing high commissions and get in first. By the time Denny found out, it would be too late.

To this end he made several attempts over the next two days to contact Mr Carpenter and to prise out of him the Parkins' documents and certificates. This industry culminated in the arrival in the office of a very tight-lipped arm of the law, who identified himself as an officer with the fraud squad.

Denny and the other long-sufferers were amused by Sean's discomfiture and sudden attack of humility. It turned out that Carpenter had disappeared a month earlier. Scrutiny of his accounts had disclosed professional theft. "Fortunately for you, Mr O'Brien, your old couple don't seem to have lost much. He hadn't really got going on them. But they are interesting to us because they appear as the last entry in his office diary; he must have visited them immediately before he went missing. Now, what can you tell us about them?"

Sean gratefully pointed out that he had spent no more than five minutes in their company. Miss Abbott, however, was a different matter…

Denny gave the police a factually accurate account of her time with the Parkins, omitting Gilbert's personal account of life in the islands in the old days. It was only after their departure that she acquainted Sean with the details of the islanders' lifestyle.

In the middle of the next week Denny went alone to see Bobby and Gilbert. For some unaccountable reason, Sean showed no interest in renewing their acquaintanceship. The house was much as Denny had remembered it, except that it smelled strongly of coconut milk, and there were bubbling sounds issuing from the kitchen.

"Connie and her sons are coming to visit us tonight, so I'm cooking up a special supper," explained Bobby. "If you remind me, I'll give you the recipe before you go."

Denny thanked Bobby and just saved herself from asking what ingredients she was using. Perhaps it was better not to know. Instead, she outlined her own ideas for their savings, and hoped they would meet with approval.

Fortunately, both Gilbert and Bobby expressed their satisfaction, and instructed her to proceed with the purchases. Gilbert smiled and remarked: "And I'm sure Denny will do a much better job for us, and a much more efficient one, than Mr Carpenter ever did."

"Oh, absolutely, Mr Parkin." Denny reassured.

Bobby nodded and said: "Do you know, Denny, we actually had the police round here, asking if we knew what had become of him? Apparently we were the last people to see him alive. I can't imagine why they thought we would know where he is."

"I don't suppose we will ever see him or the money he stole again," remarked Gilbert. "By the way, where is Mr O'Brien today?"

"He's back at the office. He sends his apologies, but he has an awful lot of work on." Denny smiled to herself. Sean had always been able to put two and two together to make five.

www.ingramcontent.com/pod-product-compliance
Ingram Content Group UK Ltd.
Pitfield, Milton Keynes, MK11 3LW, UK
UKHW020415250726
13967UKWH00007B/2654

9 781780 038483